Violet W

SATAN TOOK
A BRIDE

MILLS & BOON LIMITED
LONDON · TORONTO

First published 1975
Australian copyright 1982
Philippine copyright 1982
This edition 1982

© Violet Winspear 1975

ISBN 0 263 73923 6

Set in Linotype Baskerville 10 on 11½ pt.
02–0782

Made and printed in Great Britain by
Richard Clay (The Chaucer Press) Ltd,
Bungay, Suffolk

Mills & Boon
Best Seller Romance

A chance to read and collect some of the best-loved novels from Mills & Boon—the world's largest publisher of romantic fiction.

Every month, four titles by favourite Mills & Boon authors will be re-published in the *Best Seller Romance* series.

A list of other titles in the *Best Seller Romance* series can be found at the end of this book.

CHAPTER ONE

Toni was washing up in the kitchen of the convent; she stared into the sink and her thoughts were as filled with oddments as the water, floating about, bobbing and clinging.

How many times she had washed up the great heap of mugs and plates simply because Sister Imaculata despaired of her and said she was a tomboy and a rebel at heart, found as she had been in the *torno* of the porch, a stone wheel upon which unwanted infants were deposited, the wheel then being turned so that the baby was collected into the convent, there very often to remain if she were a girl; there to take vows of everlasting chastity and service.

A plate slipped out of Toni's hand and splashed greasy water in her face and as she wiped it away with the back of her hand her eyes held a look of rebellion that would have induced Sister Imaculata to give her a few more tasks designed to teach her humility and self-denial and a love of charity. The fact that the girl had known nothing else since being brought here wrapped in a handmade shawl didn't seem to soften the good Sister's attitude in any way at all. Toni had to be taught to be humble and to have a fearful respect for authority; the convent itself was built over the site of a very ancient house of religion which had practised so strict a code of morality that a nun had actually been entombed alive in those far-off days, for one of those sins the girls only dared whisper about in case Sister Imaculata came into the dormitory or the classroom in that quick suspicious way of hers. A woman who firmly believed in original sin and was certain that all girls were imbued with it—Toni in particular.

Perhaps it was because Toni, unlike the other girls, was Irish instead of Spanish, for when the nuns had found her, that darkening day seventeen years ago, she had been wearing a locket with a shamrock and an Irish name engraved upon it, while inside there had been a tiny pair of pictures, one of them of a man who had not possessed a Latin face.

That locket was all that Toni possessed in the world, and the Madre in charge of the convent had allowed her to have it on her seventeenth birthday, which had been two weeks ago. She had not had a party, but Sister Prudencia had baked a coconut cake and the older girls had been given a slice. Toni had been delighted to receive the locket, until Sister Imaculata had said that as she was a foundling, and the couple in the golden heart a pair of sinners, then the ornament should be sold to help pay for her keep.

The coconut cake had stuck in Toni's throat, and a resolve had taken root in her mind that day.

She wasn't a Latin girl and she didn't really belong at the Virgen de la Soledad. It wasn't only that her name was Fleet, but one look was enough to tell her that she was too much like the man in the locket to make a good and holy nun. Because the tiny images were painted she could see that he had hair like chestnuts in the sun, and eyes with lashes so long they gave the grey-green eyes a secretive look. This gave to the man's glance a seducing quality, but in Toni it was a wild, deep look which concealed the dreams and hopes she dared not express.

Because her hair was red, and such a colour was con-

6

sidered outrageous by Sister Imaculata, it had been cut as close as a boy's, as if in some way this would stop it from attracting the sun and gleaming like the copper kettles on the shelves of Sister Prudencia's kitchen.

Toni sighed and gazed beyond the kitchen window at the enclosed garden of the convent, in which were grown the potatoes, cabbages and onions which augmented the simple diet of the nuns and the forty girls for whom they cared.

It wasn't that Toni craved lobster and cream cake, like Floralia, one of the girls who was betrothed and who would be leaving soon to marry her *novio*. Toni craved something far more precious than rich food— she longed for her freedom.

It lay there in her lash-shadowed eyes, and she was at pains to hide it from the sharp and ever-vigilant glance of the Sister who now came bustling into the kitchen to see that the pile of mugs and plates had been washed and dried until they shone as speckless as the whitewashed walls of the big cool rooms and endless corridors of the convent.

There was a suspenseful moment of silence as the tall Sister stood surveying Toni at the sink. 'Again you are daydreaming, child! The tea things should be dried by now and put away in the cupboard!'

She spoke in Spanish, which Toni herself had spoken from an infant, though by the grace of the Madre she had been allowed to learn English from one of the old Sisters, who in her young days had been a member of a high-class family in Seville; well-born and wealthy Spaniards often spoke a trio of languages, and Sister Gracia had even taught Toni a smattering of French. The girl had a quick and eager mind; one that reached out beyond the boundaries of the high convent walls, inset with iron grilles like a prison.

A prison that seemed inescapable, for she had no

family and unlike some of the other girls she wasn't here to be taught lessons, or to await the claims of a *novio*, a man into whose keeping she would be released as a bride.

She was here for all time, and the terror of the thought had to be hidden from Sister Imaculata as she turned her gaze from the window and bent it upon the mugs and plates.

'Answer me, girl!' The Sister caught her by the shoulder and dug into her bones the strong fingers of a woman who had worked hard all her life. 'Are you in one of your sulky moods?'

She stared down at Toni, and there was that look in her eyes as if she wished she could cut short the girl's eyelashes as she had cut short her hair with a pair of kitchen shears.

'I'm just wondering,' said Toni, 'why I always have to do the washing up.'

'Are you, my girl? Well, it's good for your rebellious soul, and you won't need to have soft hands to please a bridegroom, will you? You do realise, Antonia, I hope, that in a while you will be taking the first of your vows, and you have to take them in a state of grace. You make me anxious, child, for you must have a humble and willing heart if you are to become a novice in the Order of the Lonely Virgin. It is just the life for you. A way to atone for the sins of your parents, and your own sin.'

'My sin?' Toni echoed. 'What have I ever done? I've been kept behind high stone walls all my life, and the only man I've ever really spoken to is Father Orazio.'

'There is no need to be insolent.' Sister Imaculata gave her a shake. 'Your sin is that you were born out of wedlock, of an unchaste mother——'

'Don't you dare speak about my mother like that!' Toni pulled free of the Sister's hand, and her young face was tormented and angry at the same time. 'At least she was loved—has a man ever loved you?'

Toni knew that she shouldn't speak in this way to a woman who had spent the best years of her life in the service of others, but it was so unfair to be picked on all the time. If she were that tall, pale, reverent girl it would be a different matter, for though Hermosa was also illegitimate, her father was known to be a well-off butcher and he was paying for her education.

No, she was a foreigner here; someone who had different colouring and ways—the black sheep who didn't fit in, and who was being forced to fit in by this woman who in Toni's eyes had the face of a female inquisitor.

Sister Imaculata stared hard at Toni, then with a rustle of coif and stiff black gown she walked to the door. 'I am going to report to the Mother Superior that you have been insolent yet again,' she said. 'And I am going to suggest that this time you be punished in a way that will hurt that pride of yours. Last time you scrubbed the stone floors of the corridors, but this time you will be confined to one of the prayer cells for twenty-four hours, to think over your insolent words in the total silence required for deep prayer and meditation. Do you hear me?'

Toni had gone white, for the prayer cells had thick walls through which not a sound could penetrate, and they were situated in the old part of the convent—the haunted part, as the girls called it, where the ghost of the entombed nun was said to wander when darkness fell.

Sister Imaculata swept from the kitchen, and Toni knew that the woman would have no softening of heart on her way to the Madre's office. She would insist that 'the foreign girl' was suitably punished this time for her lack of respect and her excess of pride, and because prayer was considered a good thing by the nuns themselves, it wouldn't occur to the Madre that a girl could be terrified by the thought of spending a day and a night alone with a ghost. The good Sisters didn't believe in ghosts, but Toni had Irish blood in her veins, and a whole lot of imagination.

What happened next might have been ordained by *el destino*, that shadowy figure in the thoughts of girls confined behind high walls, a cross between Don Juan and Saint Antony, who opened the gates of freedom and love.

Those gates were opened for Toni by a pair of *pantalones*, left hanging behind the kitchen door by the rather simple lad who came twice a week to the convent to dig the garden for the vegetables. Toni grabbed the dirty pair of jeans and fled with them into the darkening garden, where there was a certain hollow behind some cypress trees that she knew about. There a few days ago she had concealed a shirt which the gardening boy had flung off while he dug in the hot sun; she hadn't been certain of her plans at that time, but this evening she was far more certain.

It took her less than a minute to drag from her slim body the grey convent dress that just lately she had grown to hate. Against her white skin gleamed the little heart on its chain, and she briefly clenched it in her fingers and hoped wildly that the shamrock would bring her luck. Then she stepped into the jeans and did them up at the waist, and though the legs were too long this was remedied by rolling them up around her calves. She buttoned herself into the shirt, and though it smelled of tobacco smoke she preferred the smell to that of the stone walls of a prayer cell.

She shivered and fear lent speed to her heels as she shinned up one of the trees near the convent wall, an exercise she had practised in her convent dress when the opportunity had offered. On the other side of the wall lay an alley, and beyond that alley lay fields and freedom. Her problem was the drop to the ground ... if she broke a leg, then at least she wouldn't be confined to a prayer cell. But if she broke her neck ... well, Toni was Irish and she wasn't to know, ever, that her father had been a gambling man, and closing her eyes with a prayer of her own, she leapt from the convent wall and felt the rush of air as she dropped the double height of a tall man to the grass verge below the wall.

The moment she landed she knew that it had to be Saint Antony who was on her side tonight, for though the soles of her feet stung through her flat-heeled shoes, and her every bone felt shaken, she had neither broken her neck nor a leg. The grass along the verge was thick and this had acted almost as a bouncing board, and as she collected her breath, she glanced for what she hoped was the last time at the convent which had been her entire world for seventeen years. '*Vaya con Dios*,' she murmured, thinking of the girls who had been her friends. '*Adios*, and take care!'

Then she fled, running lightly into the gathering twilight, unhampered by a skirt and light on her feet because she was so slenderly built and had always been kept in greyhound condition by the amounts of scrubbing and window-cleaning she had done for Sister Imaculata. Nor had she any fear of what lay ahead of her ... the fear was behind her, there in the convent, a ghost of the past, and a phantom of the future. It had haunted her for a long time, the thought of being forced to take vows for a life for ever enclosed behind high walls. She had sometimes thought that she would rather be dead, until it had begun to enter her head that there was nothing to stop her from running away the moment the opportunity offered.

It hardly seemed to matter right now that she had no

food, no money, no prospect of shelter for the coming night. Right now she was intoxicated by a sense of freedom, and she would think about those other things when the time came.

She knew this part of the country from the various walks she and the other girls of her classroom had taken, having to walk sedately and in step, in the care of two of the Sisters, eyes downcast whenever a man came by. Not that they ever saw anyone exciting, only a farmer or two, and perhaps a swineherd with his flock. Toni would laugh then, and whisper to Floralia that they were the piglets of the Sisters, on their way to slaughter.

Toni grinned now, and gazed up at the first stars high over the fields that sloped for about five miles in the direction of the port of Santa Flavia. What lay in her mind wasn't fully distinct just yet, but like those stars that in a short while would be as clear-cut as diamonds in the plum-blue sky.

She ran for a while, then she walked, and she was too exalted by her escape to feel any sense of weariness. 'Dear St. Antony', she murmured, 'stay beside me and guard this little piglet from the clutches of Sister Imaculata. She means well, I suppose, but I'd make the worse nun in the world, and though I don't want a fat, middle-aged *novio* like poor Floralia has, it would be nice to—to have someone.'

Who that someone would be she had no idea, though she vaguely suspected that he would resemble the picture of Don Juan in that old movie magazine which one of the girls had smuggled into the convent after a visit home. He had been an actor playing the part, of course, but Toni could imagine the Don like that; tall, wickedly handsome, with a strip of dark hair across his upper lip, and the longest legs in the world. There would be a gleam of the devil in his eye, and he wouldn't be afraid of anyone; he would be completely his own master and not a soul on earth would ever tell him what to do. If they tried that on he would snap his fingers at them and go his own way without a backward glance.

On her own, now, Toni didn't glance back. She felt she would die if she was dragged back to that life of ninety-nine Latin prayers, oceans of greasy water in which floated pieces of carrot and onion, hands red and chapped from washing stone floors with strong homemade soap. She would weep her heart out, she just knew it, for this was the first time in her life that she had ever been out in the world entirely alone, with a canopy of stars above her head, and a faint tang of the sea wafting in this direction on the tail of the wind that was blowing through the thin calico shirt, which had one or two rents in it.

She ran, and then she walked a while, and as the stars grew brighter she was outlined boyishly against the skyline as the hills rose and fell in long genista-covered slopes. The lavender scent was now and again so strong that it made Toni's heart gallop, for Sister Prudencia had been fond of making lavender bags and tucking them in the deep pockets of her habit, so that when she walked by a cloud of lavender would float from her person. It was to hide the smell of onion, she always said, but Toni had long suspected that Sister Prudencia should have been a happy and bustling housewife with children of her own to cook for, and to love. The love that the good Sister had shared out among the girls at the convent was all the love that Toni had ever really known. She had no idea what any other kind of love was like ... but she felt sure that it didn't resemble the kind that would be meted out to young girls kept in seclusion until they were of an age to be wedded to their mature bridegrooms.

Toni had never been sure what was worse, being forced to become a nun, or being forced to marry a strange man. Both had seemed to her like the traps in which the gardening boy caught rabbits for the weekly stewpot.

The young runaway came to Santa Flavia around nine o'clock, tired now, and hungry, but still in an exultant mood that made light of what physical discomfort she felt after her five-mile hike across the hills.

As she came into the seaside *pueblo* she saw at once that a *fiesta* was in progress. Along the harbour were strings of coloured lights and fluttering pennants, and groups of laughing people were gathered about the stalls selling hot *churros* wrapped around long sticks, fried steaks of fish and onions, baked sweet potatoes, shellfish and all sort of fruit and candies.

Toni could smell the food, but she didn't have a *peseta* to spend, and she wandered in the crowd, her stomach churning at the aromas and the sight of people eating the crisp doughnuts and dipping their fingers into bags of chips.

Streamers entangled her boyish figure and confetti got into her close-cut hair. A trio of girls in frilled dresses, with flowers in their long coiled hair, stared at her quaint figure and laughed as they passed her by. One of them winked, and she realised that they thought her an odd sort of youth, perhaps a country yokel, too poor to be able to afford a *fiesta* costume.

Too poor to even buy an almond bun to relieve her hunger, her face pale and large-eyed in the mingling colours of the illuminations, sparkling diadems and jewelled ropes, a spangling of colour and gaiety, and the music of guitars, the flamenco and the *paso doble* performed by a girl in a lace dress with puffed underskirts and a man clad in an elegant shirt with frills down the breast, tucked into narrow-waisted trousers,

14

a stiff-brimmed hat shading his eyes.

Toni stood at the edge of the crowd and watched the performance. The Latin blood seemed hot in the veins of the couple as they wove around each other with intricate, graceful movements, arms raised as they moved towards each other, brushed and swirled apart, the frills of lace making a lovely pattern against the dark trousers of the man. The castanets were as steady and rhythmic as the beating of cicada wings, and the girl's golden hoop earrings glittered in the lights, as the man's eyes gleamed under the brim of the Andalusian hat.

It was then that the hunger, the excitement of her escape, and the scintillation of the overhead lights, caused Toni to suddenly feel as giddy as a falling moth. She clutched at the nearest object for support, and that object happened to be a stout man standing near by. Instantly, as this was a fair and the pickpockets were in town, the man thought that Toni was attempting to rob him. 'Thief!' he yelled, and he grabbed Toni by the ear and shook her so that she cried out. 'Rascal, I've caught you, haven't I? In the act!'

The man was liberally bashing her when a lean figure in a frilled shirt and a brimmed hat pushed through the crowd and ordered an end to the beating. 'You will kill the *chiquito* if you carry on like that!' The man's voice was crisp, authoritative, accustomed to obedience. 'What the devil is he supposed to have done?'

The stout man held on to Toni and glared at the tall speaker, who had been followed through the crowd by the pretty creature with whom he had been dancing. Her eyes were glittering and the castanets were still beating time on her fingers. She pressed up against the man, who abruptly pushed her away from him, a twist to his lips.

15

'He was going through my pockets,' said the stout man, looking highly offended and at the same time bitterly vengeful. 'Too much of it goes on—honest people can't come to the *fiesta* without trouble of this sort. I am taking him to the Guardia Civil——'

'Ah, but he's only a bit of a boy,' the tall man reached out and quite decisively he plucked Toni out of the grip of her tormentor. 'You don't want to see a mere child thrown into a cell. What has the *chico* taken? Have you any proof that he was picking your pocket?'

'I felt his hand on me,' the stout individual was breathing furiously from his exertions, while Toni hung in the firm grip of the *señor* and felt the pain of boxed ears, and the resentment of being called a thief in front of a crowd of people.

'I—I stumbled,' she said, her voice husky with tears. 'I wasn't after his money—I'm not a pickpocket! I'm not.'

The man who held her stared at her, and in the scintillating lights his face was strangely chiselled, just escaping the fine hand that makes men handsome and women beautiful. His eyes were odd colours—one was dark and the other was gold, and above them his brows were jet black.

'I'm inclined to believe you, *chico*,' he said at last. 'You look a bit ragged and starved, but there's something *honesto* about those eyes of yours. Take that look out of them! I'm not going to allow you to be tossed into a cell on *fiesta* night. Here, take this!' The man thrust a hand into his pocket and produced a fistful of coins, which he held out to Toni. 'Go and get yourself something to eat, and don't ever be tempted again——'

'I wasn't pinching anything, and you can keep your money!' It was the easiest and yet the hardest thing

16

Toni ever did, rejecting what this man offered so casually, because he was obviously a rich man from the cut of his clothes and the sound of his voice. Even his manner was casually arrogant, as she had always imagined that the manner of an *hombre rico* would be. Handing out advice and largesse as if it were his born privilege to do so.

Toni took a final look into those odd eyes, and then she jerked free of his hand and wriggled her way like an eel through the crowd, half pleased with herself that she had rejected his money, and half annoyed that she had allowed her pride, which she could ill afford, to rob her of her supper.

She passed a stall where the light and fluffy doughnuts were bubbling in the hot oil and the smell of the food made her stomach feel weak again. Somehow or other she just had to find a way to get a bite of food, and when a few minutes later she noticed the back entrance of a restaurant she decided to go in and ask if they needed anyone to do some washing up for a few *pesetas*. After all, she was almost up to prize-winning standard from the amount of dish-washing she had done in her time, and as she had already been taken for a boy she decided to act the boy.

Thrusting her hands into the pockets of her rolled-up jeans, she stalked into the kitchen of the restaurant, where a fat woman and a thin man were drinking wine and bemoaning the fact that they had to work while others played.

That was Toni's cue, and she grabbed it, for a single glance was enough to show her the stack of soiled dinner plates on the marble slab beside the deep sink. 'Pay me and I'll wash every single one of those, and dry them,' she said, making her voice sound gruff, and using the same rough vernacular as the gardening lad at the convent.

The man gave her a suspicious look, but the woman, whose plump face was flushed with wine and whose head was probably a bit light, was at once eager to accept the offer.

'Let him, Jorgio,' she said. 'Then you and I can go and watch the saturnalia when it begins. They'll be wearing masks and I always like that, and it's no way to spend the last night of *fiesta* week, shut up in a kitchen with other people's dirty dishes.'

'But he'll want paying——' The man swept his eyes up and down Toni's scarecrow figure. 'But not much, from the look of him. All right, *picaro*, the dishes are yours.'

'Can I have the money now?' Toni dared to ask.

'No,' said the woman. 'He might dodge out, Jorgio, so pay him when he's done the work. There's hot water in the kettle, boy, and you make sure those plates are shining or you don't get your twenty-five *pesetas*.'

'You're being a bit generous,' muttered the thin man.

'Well,' said the woman, patting her hair and making for the swing door that led towards the noise of the restaurant dining-room, 'it's *fiesta* and the poor scrap looks as if he hasn't had a square meal for days. Come on, *caro*. I fancy to get a mask and join in the fun!'

The door swung back and forth, and Toni was left alone in the garishly lit kitchen with the dirty plates and the smell of garlic. She drew a deep sigh, and then fetched the big kettle from the stove and filled the sink with the hot water. She added soda to cut the grease, and then plunged into the task that was so familiar in such unfamiliar surroundings.

The washing up took well over an hour, and by that time it was getting on for midnight, and the noise that came from the direction of the restaurant's public rooms informed her that the fun was reaching its zenith, when the masks would be removed and *fiesta* partners would see each other for the first time, if they were strangers who had met in the street and had come in here to dance to the band.

Toni was wiping her hands when the door swung open and a waiter dashed in with a tray loaded with wine glasses in which swam the dregs of red wine. 'Get these washed,' he ordered. 'We're running out!'

'But—but I'm only being paid for the plates,' Toni gasped. She was rocking on her feet, and hunger had turned to a sick feeling that she could never face food again, not after this long hour alone with the odour of grease and garlic strong in her nostrils. At the convent they had never used more than a whisper of garlic in the food, and Toni felt overpowered by the aroma.

However, she had to have her money, for it would pay for a night's lodging, but she had no intention of washing the wine glasses. She dodged past the waiter and made for the noise of the band. The fat woman had been wearing a scarlet dress under her overall, which she had taken off before joining the dancers, and Toni swayed and blinked under the whirling lights of the witchball that spun coins of coloured light over the masked couples.

She looked this way and that for the red, balloon-like dress, for the occupant of it had offered her twenty-five *pesetas* and Toni felt that she had earned every one and was determined to collect them. Wages and casual largesse were two separate things. She had borne the grease and the smell of garlic in order to earn the money, and with a desperate set to her pale young face Toni began to push through the circle of a *sardana*, with the couples taking the short, then the long steps that tossed her back and forth like a piece of flotsam.

'Get away, boy!' It became a sort of game, and the masked dancers began to add spice to the saturnalia as they pushed Toni from one side of the circle to the other. The laughter became mocking and wild, and the girl felt as if she had suddenly plunged into a nightmare. She knew it was just a game, an excess of *fiesta* spirits, aided by the strong red wine of the region, but her emotions were too strung, too on the edge of exhaustion for the fun to be other than a torment for her.

Someone pushed her with exuberant roughness, and with a cry she felt herself falling ... falling beneath the dancing feet, the sharp heels of the women and the heavy soles of the men.

'Watch out!' someone said. 'The little scarecrow will be hurt!'

She felt the kick from someone's shoe, striking her temple with a sharp and shocking pain ... then she knew nothing as the witchball flared into a dazzle of flame and emerald light, extinguished by a total darkness.

CHAPTER TWO

THE room was lamplit, revealed slowly to Toni as her wits returned to her. She lay there and could have sworn that she heard the sound of the sea ... nonsense, it had to be part of the effect of being kicked in the head, which she remembered at once because the fear she had felt as she fell beneath the dancing feet was still with her.

She gave a little gasp as the fear gripped her and at once a figure came to the side of the bed, and she gasped again as she saw a face in a black mask bending over her; a dominant nose jutted from under the edge of the mask and the mouth was emphasised in clear-cut lines that might have been faintly cruel. The lines of the jaw were lean and dark, deep-clefted, as if this man often smiled with irony at the vagaries of life.

At any other time Toni would have noticed the distinctive face, but right now her attention was caught by the mask ... her heart thumped and she thought to herself that she was looking at Mephistopheles himself ... the devil who had no love of the light and who jeered at people.

'So you are back among the living,' he drawled, and he leaned over Toni and taking her face in his lean-fingered hand turned her head and quizzed her bruised temple. 'That will be a mixture of colours for the next few days, and I imagine you have quite a headache?'

She nodded, and then stiffened from head to foot as the lean fingers proceeded to take hold of the shirt that she wore and to examine the tears in it and the marks made by the earth-stained fingers of the gardening lad to whom it really belonged.

'You're about the dirtiest little object that ever came aboard the *Miranda*, and that will have to be remedied as soon as possible. Well, *golfo*, do you think you could keep down a tot of brandy? It will steady your nerves and ease some of that head pain.'

Golfo ... little ragamuffin. Toni relaxed slightly, and stopped being so shocked that this man should so casually touch her. He believed her to be a boy, so that was all right. Toni had spent too many years in a convent to know that it might not have been all right, if this masked man had been as odd as his eyes through the slanting openings of the mask. She stared up at him, recognition dawning on her face, which she wasn't to know was as grubby as the clothes she had on.

'So now you recognise me, eh?' He pulled off the mask and tossed it to one side, and his black brows had a sardonic twist as he studied the youthful figure in the bed that was attached to the wall of a fairly spacious ship's cabin.

Toni lay on the blue coverlet and a pillow had been plumped so that her head was slightly raised. The light of the fixed lamp slanted across her face, which was puckish with her slanting grey eyes haunted by green lights, her hungry bones and pointed chin. Thin and quick as a needle, she was vulnerable as a fawn, a colt, anything wild and innocent. There was no hint of her slight curves under the shirt that was a couple of sizes too large for her, and if her ankles had a delicate shape to them, the man who quizzed her from head to foot did no more than give them a cursory glance.

'You look as if you might pass out again, so have that brandy and a bite of food.' The lean figure in the close-cut pants and the frilled shirt walked to a cabinet that stood against a wall, and when he opened it there was the gleam of a tantalus and the clink of wine glasses. 'I shall join you, *golfo*. It isn't every day that I rescue a waif from a saturnalia. How in the name of the devil did you come to be part of that? They were having a real game with you, weren't they, scrap?'

He returned to the bed with a pair of glasses in his hands, and in each one there gleamed the golden *coñac*. 'Can you sit up without my help?' He placed one of the glasses on the bedside cabinet.

'Yes——' Toni struggled into a sitting position and felt her head give a painful thump. A slight groan escaped her, and at once her host sat down on the side of the bed and before Toni could protest he pulled her into the crook of his arm and put the rim of her glass to her lips.

'Sip it, *golfo*, and don't you dare lose any of it. It's part of a consignment smuggled out of France; a bullfighting friend of mine is fond of his brandy, but rich as he is from his killings he doesn't care to pay the exorbitant tax on the stuff. Good, eh?'

Toni felt the aromatic warmth on her lips and on its way down her throat ... she had never tasted spirit in her life before, and to her surprise she found it very pleasant and as she finished off the brandy felt her eyes grow pleasurably heavy and hazy.

'*Muy bueno*,' she said, her voice a little slurred. 'I've never had it before.'

'From the look of you, *golfo*, it's very apparent that you've never had much of anything.' With the faintest of frowns Toni's host reached for his own glass, but he treated the fine brandy with more consideration, and Toni watched him with reflective grey eyes as he sniffed at the aroma of the brandy, swirled it once or twice in the glass, and drank it with slow appreciation.

'That, *chico*, is how a gentleman drinks his brandy, and among other things I have been called a *señor* in my time.' The odd eyes that imparted such an odd sensation to anyone upon whom they dwelt for any length of time dwelt dark and gold upon Toni. 'Are you going to tell me your name, and how you came to be mixed up in the saturnalia?'

'It—it just happened, *señor*. I was washing up in the kitchen there, and the people who were supposed to pay me were in the crowd somewhere. I—I was looking for them, and then the dancers began to make fun of me.' Toni flushed at the memory, half with annoyance, and half with humiliation that she should cut such a figure of fun. The fear had receded and she vaguely knew that it had something to do with this man. It was instinctive, for no one had ever taught her or told her that certain men were naturally of a different species from other men; that they were a focus for all eyes, at the centre of things without really being a part of them. That they were paid homage as if it were a right, and that they made their own laws and lived by them. It was inborn, magnetic, and this man had it, a power of personality that made other people instinctively obey him.

She couldn't remember being carried away from the restaurant, but she guessed that this man had done it, dragged her clear of the stamping feet and brought her to his—home?

Toni looked around her, and her eyes widened as she saw the portholes with the curtains half pulled, the gleam of panelled walls, the austerity and yet the subtle hint of luxury imparted by the carpet and the divan beside a bookcase.

'Oh!' She flung a hand against her lips. 'Is this a ship?'

'I like to think so,' he drawled. 'It's the *Miranda*, and it's my yacht and sizeable enough for a bachelor and his crew and a captain. We lifted anchor out of Santa Flavia over an hour ago, and we are on the high seas. It has a good feeling to it—what do you say, *golfo*?'

As he asked this question, his eyes narrowed until they seemed to flicker with a strange and reckless fire. Toni gripped the bedcover and realised that some angel, or devil, had answered her prayer and seen to it that she was never to see the Convent of the Lonely Virgin ever again.

'What are you?' her host demanded. 'A gipsy boy from the *triano*, sent out to pick pockets——?'

'I wasn't doing any such thing,' she said indignantly.

'Perhaps not.' He shrugged. 'A gipsy is cleverer at it than you appeared to be. Have you any family?'

She shook her head. 'Not a soul,' she said, and it was the truth. Her mother had disowned her long ago, and it wasn't possible to ever think of nuns as foster-mothers. They were too devout to have normal, sensual feelings of love.

'And what are you called?' As he spoke Toni's host reached for a cigar-box on the bedside cabinet. It had a *Romeo y Julieta* picture on the front, like one of those in which Floralia had kept a string of beads which her *novio* had sent to her. Toni watched, for she had never seen this before, the selection of a thin dark cigar, the striking of a match, the application of the flame to the leafy cylinder. Smoke came sharp and blue from the sculptured nostrils, and Toni breathed it in.

'Want to have a puff?'

'No—*gracias*.' She shook her head.

'You'd like some food, eh? And I ask again, what are you called?'

'Toni,' she said. 'Toni Fleet.'

'It's an Irish name.' He narrowed his odd eyes against the smoke. 'What is an Irish ragamuffin doing in Spain, and speaking the language as if born to it?'

'I was born in Spain,' she explained. 'I—I was brought up in a house in the country and I—I worked for the gardener there. Digging, and other things.'

'Show me your hands.'

It was a definite order and she obeyed it, watching those black and expressive eyebrows draw together as her rough, red-fingered young hands were studied.

'They worked you well, eh?' That strange glance flashed over her face. 'A middle-aged charwoman might be proud of those hands. Did you suddenly decide to run away?'

'Yes, *señor*. I—I wanted to be independent. I'm not afraid of hard work—you should have seen the pile of washing up I did before I—well, got that kick in the head.' She bit her lip. 'What will you do with me? Throw me off at the next port of call?'

'I might,' he said. 'It all depends.'

'Depends on what, *señor*?' Because she had never learned the art of seduction Toni couldn't be anything else but candid with a man, and in that moment there was a boyish tilt to her chin, a steady questioning in her grey eyes. All she asked for was a straight answer, and a slight smile flickered on the lips of the man who looked at her.

'If you'd be prepared to be cabin-boy on this trip. Running about after me, taking my orders, but not getting under my feet. Could you do that? It might make a change from the—digging.'

'Do you—do you mean it?' Toni felt that she had to be dreaming ... cabin-boy to this strange personage, whose face in the smoke of his cigar was somehow baroque and faintly sinful, not at all like the placid and kindly countenance of Father Orazio.

'I always mean what I say,' he said. 'There is no logic in building up hopes only to kick them down. My cruelties are far more subtle than that, so beware, boy! I can be cruel when I'm in the mood!'

'I am sure you can,' she said, for in a convent an inmate learns to be entirely truthful, or very devious, and Toni preferred the truth to fabrications because courage and truth and a little gold locket were the only real possessions she ever had in her life.

'You may be frank with me,' drawled her host, 'but not damned cheeky, do you hear? A saint likes to be told what he is, but a sinner is a bit touchy. You can see, can't you, that I'm not a patient man, or a very kind one? You aren't a fool, for all that you look a bit simple. I'm going to the galley to get you a bowl of soup and some bread, and while I've gone you can absorb what I have said to you. My name, by the way, is Luque de Mayo, and a string of other appellations there is no need for your bruised head to try and memorise. I shall call you Toni, and any other names that suit my mood, and you may call me Señor Luque.' Cigar smoke clouded about the dark eye and the gold eye as the *señor* rose from the bedside on his long legs and towered lean and dark over the very new addition to his crew. His smile was enigmatic and suited to his cynical face. His shirt was intensely white against his almost Arab-dark skin; he had a very arresting quality, almost insolent in its strength, and careless possession of power. His motives for any action would always be deep, dark and dangerous, and had Toni been older, more worldly, less trained to obey, she would have fled him as Rhea fled Mars when she strayed into the night and met him.

He turned and went from the cabin, walking as he had danced the *paso doble*, with Iberian grace and a certain tigerishness.

He left Toni all alone in the cabin, yet with her thoughts alive with him. The way he looked, the way he spoke, the way he took charge of her . . . like one of those dark kings out of the old courts of Andalusia. A convent virgin as she was, she didn't pause to wonder what he would have done with her had he known her true identity. But he thought her a boy, and so he offered her a job in his yacht. She was achingly grateful to him . . . she knew then and there that if he ever kicked her like a dog, she would never cease to be his slave.

It was an odd thought, and she gnawed her knuckles, and was still doing it when the cabin door swung open and he returned, carrying a circular bar tray with a china bowl on it that steamed and smelled very good indeed. With the soup he brought a twist of Spanish bread, and a spoon.

'There's no need to eat those unlovely hands of yours,' he chided, in that voice that was richly grating and mocking. 'I'm quite sure they'd taste as awful as they look. This is hot onion soup, and I hope you like it.'

Toni had often had onion soup, but as soon as she tasted this particular bowl she knew how rich and different it was from that thin and colourless brew from the convent kitchen. She ate as if she were starved, and all the time Luque de Mayo watched her, almost as if some new species of creature had come into his orbit, to amuse him for a while.

'Would you care for some more?' he asked, when the last crumb of bread had disappeared through Toni's hungry lips. 'I'll have an omelette made for you if you like?'

'No, *gracias, señor*.' Toni sank back against the pillow replete. 'I'm most grateful for the soup—it was delicious. The best I've ever tasted.'

'What did they feed you on at this—house?' He lounged against the foot of the bed and on his face there was that quizzical, intrigued, partly amused look of having stumbled on a new sort of game. 'The left-overs from the table, *golfo*? You know, I'm not sure that I ought to take you off on a voyage without some sort of permission from someone, Even a bit of rag and bone like you has a guardian of sorts—just how old are you, by the way?'

'I was seventeen a fortnight ago,' she told him. 'I'm old enough to please myself what I do and—oh, please, I don't want to go back—there. You won't make me go back, will you?'

'Not if you're that desperate to get away from the place.' His eyes ran over her ruffled hair, cut as if under a pudding basin, and bright as tinted leaves against the white pillow. 'You really are the oddest scrap of humanity that ever came my way, and though I'm not the most benevolent of men I don't disregard the distress of young animals, and you're no more than that, in a way. An unwanted young pup, who has taken a dislike to its owner and is after a new one. So, *golfo*, you want me for your new owner? And why, I wonder?'

'Well,' she said, and realised that she was going to have to get used to being referred to as a pup and a ragamuffin, 'you brought me here, didn't you? I didn't ask in the first place to come aboard your yacht. I was unconscious when you hoisted anchor and set sail.'

'True,' he agreed. 'I had told the captain to hoist anchor on the stroke of midnight and being a man of the sea he always does what he's told. It was striking midnight as I came aboard with you—do you believe in *el destino*?'

'Yes.' She spoke with a low-voiced fervency.

'Superstitious, eh?' His smile was faintly derisive, and his eyelids slanted across the oddly matched eyes that would always make him unforgettable.

'Aren't you, *señor*?' Toni retaliated. 'You're a Spaniard.'

'I'm that, and several sorts of other things, as you will learn, *picaro*. It's settled, then, you are taken on as cabin-boy and you will answer to me and no one else. The steward can be a bit of a tartar, so he will be informed that he isn't to box your ears for any misdeed, for that is my privilege. Furthermore we can't have you sleeping here in my cabin, or the rumour might get around that my dash of English blood has corrupted the Latin in me.'

'English?' she echoed, unaware of the implications in the rest of his remark. 'But you don't look——'

'No, I don't, do I?' His drawl was at its most sardonic. 'All I have to show for having an English mother is a gold eye, as you will no doubt have noticed. Now hop out of my bed, *pronto*, and I'll show you where you can sleep.'

Toni slid off the bed, feeling slightly unsteady as she stood up, but otherwise all right. Her head was still aching, but she had borne worse aches at the convent after spending hours on her knees scrubbing the long corridors. Besides, she was aboard the *Miranda*, and the owner of it was a strange and wonderful personage, like no other adult she had ever known. She doubted if he had ever said a prayer in his life, and yet she had the feeling that he would go through fire and roaring water for what he did believe in.

She followed him from the big cabin into a small one attached to it. Plain, spotless, smelling of polished wood and brass, with a Spanish throwover across the narrow bunk-bed.

'This is where my valet would normally sleep,' said

Luque de Mayo. 'But when I go sailing I don't care to be too formal, and I can manage to dress myself. Do you think you could sleep here and not make a pest of yourself when I don't need you? There are books on that shelf near the bed, if you can read. Can you?'

'Of course!' Toni looked around her and was very pleased by what she saw. All her life she had shared a dormitory with other girls, and now at last she would sleep in a room of her own. She could have thrown her arms around her new master and hugged him, but that wasn't quite the correct behaviour for a boy. At all costs Luque de Mayo had to go on believing she was a young male. Somehow she knew that it would be dangerous, one way or the other, if he discovered that he had a girl on his yacht. She had seen him dancing at the *fiesta*, and she had seen the danger in him when he was with a woman.

There wasn't a lot that Toni knew about love between men and women, only what had been whispered in her ear by those girls at the convent who had *novios* waiting for them to grow up a little. It had all struck her as being rather tasteless ... it would be much more fun to go on being a boy ... cabin-boy on this swift-running yacht, already miles from Santa Flavia and the convent.

'I'm very grateful to you, *señor*, for taking me on like this,' she said, and she thrust her hands into the pockets of the earth-stained *pantalones*, and was possibly the most comic figure that Luque de Mayo had ever surveyed in his life.

'We shall have to rig you out with some clothes,' he said drily. 'Those rags can be slung overboard. Anyway, it's late and you're rocking on your feet, so the matter of an outfit can be left until the morning. Do you sleep in your skin, or do you want a pair of pyjamas—though, come to think of it, mine would

31

fit you a couple of times over. Just a jacket ought to do you, eh?'

He strode off, leaving Toni alone in the small cabin. Through the adjoining door which was left open she saw him pull open a drawer of the polished chest and take from it a garment, which when handed to Toni proved to be a dark silk pyjama jacket with a scarlet dragon-like figure embroidered on the breast pocket.

'That is a salamander,' he told her, when she glanced at the figure. 'It's part of the family device— the part I took for my own.'

'The salamander isn't afraid of fire, is he?' Toni traced the device with her fingers.

'He's a bit of a hellish-looking creature, and that's why, in all probability, he likes the flames of hell.' Luque de Mayo looked utterly cynical as he spoke those words, and Toni knew that he referred to himself and not the fire dragon. 'So it's settled, *golfo*, you will sail under my colours, and do my bidding, and be warned that my disposition is like my eyes—almighty odd!'

He swung to the door, where he paused to add: 'There's a bathroom at the other side of my cabin. I'd prefer you to use that rather than the one used by the crew. *Buenas noches, golfo.*'

'*Buenas noches, señor.*'

The door closed behind him, and Toni was left alone with the lingering memory of his enigmatic smile.

She undressed beside the bed, with the lamp turned out, and only the pale wash of the stars through the porthole. She could hear the water like rustling silk against the sides of the yacht, and she didn't know where they were going, but through her mind ran the words of that other Miranda in Shakespeare's play ... the one she had read with Sister Gracia not so long ago. 'This is a new-born world and full of strange delights.'

Strange delights, and strange tiny fears, that made her clamber quickly into bed, clad in the dark silk jacket that reached to her thighs, and felt so luxurious against her skin, which had never known the touch of real silk before.

She lay there in the dark, feeling the swift and powerful motion of the yacht. Only a couple of times in her life had she seen the sea, and now here she was adrift on all those limitless miles of deep water, by grace of a man who hinted that he had a graceless soul. Toni fiercely told herself that she didn't care if he was as bad as the devil ... but all the same she had better climb out of bed again and say her prayers. She had been saying them on her knees for too long now to be able to discard the habit overnight, and with a pale gleam of slim legs she climbed out of the bunk-bed and knelt on the tufted rug that half-covered the floor.

She was there like that, hands clasped and eyes tightly shut, when the light near the door sprang the little cabin back into brightness again. Toni turned a startled head, blinking those long lashes of her grey-green eyes as the sudden light dazzled her.

Luque de Mayo stood by the door staring at her. In his hand he carried a china mug. 'What the devil are you doing?' he asked.

Toni scrambled to her feet, and the jacket of his pyjamas hung round her slight body and concealed what curves she had. But minus the shirt and trousers of the gardening lad, which had had a rough grubbi-ness about them, she took on a look that made the strange eyes of her host go narrow and probing.

'Were you praying, pretty boy?' he gibed. 'That's one for the books, a little ragamuffin with nothing and no one, down on his knees giving thanks. Thanks for what, Toni? For being here with me?'

'Perhaps,' she muttered. 'You have everything and you are someone, so you wouldn't know what it feels like to feel thankful—for the job, for the bed, for not having to spend the night in some doorway, for I don't suppose I'd have got my money for all that washing up.'

'Likely as not you'd have been kicked out for your pains. Here!' He came to her, this man who jeered at her for saying a prayer. 'Onion soup always gives me a thirst, so I thought you might like a mug of tea. Hot and sweet, *chico*, the way love ought to be.'

Big-eyed, bewildered by him, Toni accepted the steaming mug. The neck of his shirt was open against his dark skin, and even to her innocent eyes he had a look of unholy attraction. His strange eyes glittered as once again he looked her up and down.

'It's a wonder all that work didn't kill you,' he drawled. 'There's not much of you, is there? You're all eyes, Toni. They're large enough to swallow the world, and they're filled with a thousand questions. I think, young one, that life might just be on the verge of beginning for you. Seventeen, eh? Can you guess how old I am?'

'Between thirty and forty,' she said.

'Exactly.' He grinned. 'I've lived two lives while you have been living one, and I've been round the world a couple of times. I have no beliefs and I wouldn't know how to pray, for I have worshipped in the temples of the half-gods, *chico*. My English relatives refuse to know me, and in Spain I am a scandal because I was the co-respondent in a notorious divorce case. I have only one home where I can be halfway at peace—this yacht, Toni, with the sea between me and the world. The sea can be cruel, *golfo*, but not half as

34

cruel as people. The sea can be lonely, but not half so lonely as a crowd.'

With a lithe, dark grace Luque de Mayo turned on his heel and went away, switching off the light so that Toni was left alone in the darkness to sip her tea and to think over what he had said. All her life she had heard about sin and hell, but never before had she seen them reflected in a pair of eyes.

Dark sin in the left eye, and a promise of sheerest gold in the right one. They were the soul of the man, as conflicting as he was. A half-god who sat over the cards and wine, the women and the song, until he turned to the sea where he could live and breathe again.

Toni finished her tea and crept beneath the covers of her bed ... she would be his cabin-boy, his page, his Ganymede. As a boy she could be with him, perhaps for always. As a girl she could have but an hour or a night of his life, and that was all.

She would have to be very careful that he didn't find her out as a girl ... a convent virgin who had run away before she could become a reluctant nun.

Whatever would the good Sister Imaculata have to say if she could see now the young rebel whom she had tried to make into a little saint? Clad in a man's pyjama jacket, and that man a self-confessed sinner! Dear and terrible Sister Imaculata, who would probably say that it had been preordained for the foreign girl to fall into the hands of the devil himself.

CHAPTER THREE

IN all probability Luque de Mayo was so unpredictable that those who knew him as well as anyone was able to know him were not surprised when he did the unexpected.

The captain and crew of the *Miranda* didn't show a great deal of surprise that their numbers had been swelled, very slightly, by a cabin boy. But the door stood ajar between Toni's small cabin and that of her host, employer, master (she didn't quite know how to regard him yet) and she heard what the captain had to say about the matter when he came to discuss their charting for the day.

'These street arabs are all thieves, *señor*, so if you're set on having him aboard, then you had better put him under my wing and he can sleep in the crew's quarters. If you pander to him, he'll start being impudent and then you'll regret your good nature.'

Toni, listening with avid ears behind the door, heard Luque de Mayo give a scoffing laugh. 'I have no good nature to speak of, Martelo, but in this case there's something—I don't know—a dash of good blood in the bundle of rags and I have a notion to do a spot of training. He's had it a bit rough, but he isn't a whipped little cur and I won't have him bullied by the steward, who does a fine job of keeping the yacht in order but who isn't over-sensitive when it comes to people.'

'You regard that in there as people?' There was an

amazed note in the captain's voice. 'Southern Spain is full of the likes of that lad, who's more than likely the by-blow of some *caballero*. Oh indeed, the dash of good blood will show itself in the face, but these urchins usually take after their gipsy mothers. Hand him over to me, *señor*. I'll see to it that he isn't bullied, but he will be better off in the forecastle, if he's going to learn to be useful on a ship.'

'Do you imagine I shall spoil him, Martelo?' Cheroot smoke drifted lazily in the direction of Toni's cabin, and she visualised those odd eyes upon that partly open door, left that way after a cup of coffee and a jam roll had been left at her bedside. 'That will make a change for the little beggar, to be spoiled. He looks as if all his life he's been—how shall I put it? Held on a chain, until he finally snapped it and cut loose. Leave him to me, Martelo. If he starts getting cheeky, then I shall soon slap him down.'

The captain laughed sardonically at that, as if he rather doubted the ability of Luque de Mayo to slap down a bit of a kid. 'Am I to have a look at him, *señor*? He had a knock on the head, didn't he? Has he recovered his wits yet?'

'Without a doubt.' The drawling voice, with that attractive grating sound to it, that dash of cultured English mixed with Castilian, drew near to Toni's door, and she drew back hastily against the side of the bunk-bed and was standing there when the two men entered. The captain of the yacht wasn't so tall as the master of it, but with his dark beard and his uniform he had a stern look of authority that made Toni inordinately grateful to Luque de Mayo for not consigning her to the captain's charge.

She stood there, still clad in the silk pyjama jacket because her clothes had been taken away and no doubt fed to the fishes. Her heart beat fast and furiously under the dark silk, and she was shockingly aware of her imposture and had to control a panicky urge not to duck back into the bed and hide herself.

As the captain swept his stern look over her, she cast an imploring look at Luque de Mayo, who this morning was clad in black levis and a black, high-throated sweater that made him look like a panther, who walked with equal silence and suppleness as he came to her and with a single strong movement lifted her and tossed her back in bed.

'Have a lie in,' he said. 'I doubt if it's a luxury you've ever enjoyed.' He pulled the sheet up about her, then turned to look at the other man. 'What do you make of him, Martelo?'

'That's a nasty bruise,' grunted the captain. 'How on earth did he get it—in a fight?'

'People were treading all over him, as usual.' Luque de Mayo gave her a quick look. 'Isn't that so, *golfo*?'

She nodded, her eyes fixed upon his lean left hand as he took the cheroot from his lips and a fine thread of smoke drifted up over his dark, distinctive features. She felt—curiously—that she wanted to take that hand and kiss it. She didn't suppose him kind, but he had a mysterious way of knowing her mind, and he treated her as if she were a small animal who had to be coaxed to trust people. A little animal which he had a mind to treat as a pet for a while. Lord help her, she thought, if she ever bit the hand that fed her.

'He can stay there for a while, but he'll want something to wear when he gets up. What have we in store, Martelo? Anything that can be cut down to size? My pants are a lot too long in the leg.'

'I'll find him something.' The captain stood frowning at Toni's tousled cap of hair and the lightness of her skin that the Spanish sun had never fully tanned because the high walls of the convent had shut so much of it out. 'He's an odd one for the south to have spawned, *señor*. What is he called?'

'Toni Fleet,' drawled the man who had picked her up off the floor of a tavern and carried her off Spanish soil on to his yacht. It was what a man might do with a puppy dog!

'Irish eyes,' grunted the captain. 'A rebellious clan if ever there was one. Does your head hurt you, boy?'

'A bit,' she admitted. Her head ached and when she touched her temple even slightly it felt sore. When she had gone to the bathroom a short while ago she had noticed in the mirror the extent of the bruising; she knew that it was because of her whiteness of skin that she bruised so dramatically, but the look of her battered temple had the effect of softening the captain's brusque manner.

'Yes, I'd recommend a rest,' he said. 'Then perhaps a breath of air on deck to perk you up for some work—'

'He won't be doing any work just yet.' Luque de Mayo spoke lazily but with an underlying note of firmness in his voice. 'It isn't pleasant being kicked about, is it, *golfo*?'

'No, especially after all that washing up,' she muttered. It still rankled, not being paid her due for all that greasy work on an empty stomach. At the convent the girls were told that they worked for the Lord, but it was a different matter doing work in a tavern for nothing!

'For heaven's sake forget that pile of dirty dishes.' Luque de Mayo gave an exasperated laugh. 'That's over with! Can't you get it into your funny head?'

'Not really.' She looked at him for wonderment, for it just seemed too good to be true that her days of dirty dish washing were actually finished with. She could hope and pray that he would keep her with him, but life wasn't made up of miracles.

'As you're so fond of water, then you can watch it from up on deck—later on, of course, when Captain Martelo has arranged about some togs for you. There's just one thing——' Ash had collected on the cheroot and with a slight mutter of impatience Luque de Mayo strode to the porthole and tipped it outside. 'Don't fall overboard, will you? I don't want to make a habit of coming to your rescue.'

'I'll be good,' she said quickly. 'I don't want to cause you any bother, *señor*.'

'But that's the trouble with young pups,' he drawled, 'they can be bothersome. Do you swim?'

She shook her head, for the good Sisters had never considered it a requisite for anyone entering the enclosed life to be a swimmer. The water she had mainly seen had been in buckets and sinks!

'Then you'll have to be taught, some time or other, just in case we ever run into high water and peril.'

'Don't invite trouble by talking like that, *señor*.' Captain Martelo frowned so that his face seemed all dark brows and beard.

'Ah, you're all sailor and Spaniard, aren't you?' Luque de Mayo gave that ironical laugh of his and flicked the remainder of his cheroot into the sea beyond the porthole. 'Superstitious and always on the lookout for the evil eye. It's a wonder you care to sail the yacht of someone like me!'

'Someone like you, *señor*?' The captain looked puzzled.

'People in Spain have been known to cross themselves when I have crossed their path.' That drawl was at its most grating and cynical as Luque de Mayo flung up a hand and indicated his eyes. '*Mal ojos*, wouldn't you say? Evil eyes?'

Toni, there in the bunk-bed, with her knees drawn up beneath the covers and her arms wrapped around them, stared at Luque de Mayo and wondered how she dared to give herself into his keeping when he did look as if he could be—no, not evil, but sinister and tricky, and cruel when the mood was on him. Spaniards would cross themselves, yet he, too, was more of the south than of the north, with his skin that was dark golden, and his black hair that peaked sharply above his strange eyes. No one would ever take him for half-English, even though he used a species of slang that made his speech both colourful and cosmopolitan.

He, too, was a rebel, she thought. He rebelled against Spanish tradition that expected him, who was obviously high-born, to behave as an aloof *hidalgo* and not a sailor of the high seas, smuggling *coñac* out of France for his bullfighting friends, and dancing the *paso doble* in the streets of San Flavia. In England he would never be accepted as an Englishman, not with his Latin looks and his tendency to collect the admiration of women as the coat of a donkey collected burrs.

He's a bit like me, she decided. A fish out of water—in his case a tiger-shark out of the dangerous depths of an ocean she had not yet plumbed.

'Stop staring!' Fingers snapped under Toni's nose, and she gave a start that sent her toppling back against the pillow. Captain Martelo had gone from the cabin, and she was alone with Luque de Mayo. He gazed down at her, and then very lightly he put a finger against her temple.

'What big eyes you have, *golfo*.'

Her heart thumped, at his touch, and at the narrowing of his eyes.

'Hurts, eh?'

She nodded, and guessed that she had gone rather wan and white. He mustn't discover the game that she was playing, for she'd be no match for his annoyance, and for that other tendency that lurked in self-willed

41

men who got mixed up in notorious divorce scandals.

'Well, the pain will fade away as the bruise fades, *golfo*. The heel of that woman marked you well, didn't it? That's the way of women, to leave their mark, and it isn't always a pretty one.' The long fingers slid beneath Toni's chin and he tilted her face to him. 'Kicked in the face by a woman, and not even at the shaving stage, eh?'

The mockery was rampant on the lean, chiselled face that by some miracle had escaped being handsome and was, instead, as fascinating as the face of Lucifer must have been when he was tossed out of the celestial regions into the infernal ones.

'You a slow starter?' Luque de Mayo mocked. 'I had my first girl when I was fifteen—she offered herself on a plate and I was at the curious stage. Ah, what's that look you're giving me? Are you shocked, you puritanical little street urchin?'

'I—I've never had the chance to be anything else——'

'What, an urchin?'

'No—a puritan.'

Luque de Mayo laughed at that, in his deep-pitched, grating way, so that his laughter seemed a mixture of spice and ground-glass. 'The hell you have, with your hand in a fat man's pocket?'

'Y-you keep saying that,' she protested, 'and all I did was stumble against him. I felt dizzy—I was so hungry——'

'The devil you were!' The mockery was wiped off the lean face as the mask last night had been pulled from the features stamped with *hidalgo* and rake. 'That's one experience I can't brag about, that I've ever gone so hungry I lost my balance. You poor scrap! Come into my stateroom and take breakfast with me. I protest against the Latin coffee and a bun, and shrimps at eleven o'clock. I enjoy bacon and eggs, and lashings of butter on my bread. Come, out of the bed with you!'

He tossed aside the covers and his arms had hold of her, swinging her clear of the bed, and the floor, as he carried her into the spacious cabin with the circular table and the divan, and the drop-flap desk, and the fitted wardrobe. All the requirements of a sailing gentleman, who had now acquired a pet puppy to tease.

Toni, who was no puppy but a girl of seventeen, whose adult feelings were beginning to give her trouble each time this man touched her, was desperately relieved when he dropped her to the divan and allowed her to drag the pyjama jacket down over her knees. She caught him with a smile at the edge of his lips, then he swung to the table, where a covered silver tray waited to be explored. He lifted the cover and the smell of bacon and eggs wafted to Toni, along with the smell of toast and coffee.

'One of the best aromas in the world,' he drawled. 'Almost better than wax polish, the smell of wine jasmine, and the cool scent of a woman's skin.'

He proceeded to load up a plate for Toni, adding drily: 'Once we get some flesh on you, *golfo*, you might begin to attract a bit of love life. Has there never been any love in your life?'

'Not really, *señor. Gracias.*' She accepted the plate of delicious-looking food which he handed to her, slices of crisp bacon, plump kidneys, tiny mushrooms, and eggs flamenco. She gazed at the food with wide eyes, for never in her life had she seen so much food on a single plate; food that started the day and was not reckoned the mainstay, that had to last until thin barley coffee and a slice of bread at suppertime.

'You've been starved of several things, haven't you,

Toni?' He handed her a bottle with sauce in it. 'Only add a little of that—you don't want to smother the taste of the food.'

'Please——' She swallowed the lump in her throat. 'Don't watch me—you make me feel peculiar.'

'Do I?' he drawled, starting on his own breakfast. 'You intrigue me, *chico*, that's all. It may be good for my black soul to befriend a pup like you, for you've had several kinds of cans tied to your young tail, and I'm wondering what kind of a young dog you'll grow into now the cans have been left behind you. Eat up! Fried food is delectable when hot, but rather awful when it gets cold—like a love affair that starts with a sizzle and ends with a whimper.'

'I—I wouldn't know,' she said, forking bacon and mushroom into her mouth and finding the taste as relishing and rare as being here with a man who looked and talked like no one else in the world. 'I suppose you could say, *señor*, that when it comes to—to that kind of thing, I'm very backward.'

'You mean you're a virgin,' he said crisply. 'Well, don't apologise for it, Toni. You save yourself for the right—person, and don't tear any pages out of my book. My book of life isn't exactly a pretty one, and in lots of respects I'm not a very suitable owner for an impressionable young pup. Martelo would have hoisted you off to the forecastle if I had let him——'

'Oh, I'm glad you didn't, *señor*.' She gave him a look that for a moment was quite unguarded and filled with hero-worship, and at once the face of Luque de Mayo took on a derisive and mocking expression.

'Don't put me on any pedestals, youngster. I do things to suit myself, and when they no longer suit me I get shot of the object or the idea that took my fancy for a while. I'm what they call fickle. I'm like my own eyes, *golfo*, neither one thing nor the other. I can be a gipsy, or I can be a gentleman, according to my mood. You'll learn, Toni, you with your affections as ungainly as your limbs which haven't yet come to terms with this quickly moving world of ours. Don't worship saints or sinners, for both demand your soul, and each man's soul should be his own.'

Toni listened avidly as she ate the food he provided, an odd young figure there on the wide leather divan, with its dark blue cushions embroidered with the red salamander. The sun was slanting through the port-holes and her hair was attracting the bright rays, so that every now and again Luque de Mayo flicked his eyes across her head, and something amused and speculative would glint in their depths.

'Who, I wonder, taught you to be a good listener?' he drawled, lounging back in his seat to light one of the lethal-looking cheroots that he seemed to smoke at regular intervals. 'Does my cynical philosophy make sense to you, or is your mouth too full for any sort of comment? No, don't stop eating, *chico*. Finish that peach, and the figs.'

He lounged there, eyelids drooping over his odd eyes as the smoke of his cheroot drifted into the sunlit air of the cabin, which smelled of food and a tang of salt from the ocean. Which had a masculine air, both comfortable and private . . . a sanctum which made Toni wonder if she was the first female to ever invade what Luque de Mayo kept for his very own; something apart from that other life that he led.

Peach juice shone on her lips as she cast a look at him from beneath her lashes, and he gave her a tan-talising smile tinged with irony. 'I wonder what I shall do with you?' The murmur drifted to Toni along with the smoke. 'I suppose I could become your guard-ian and send you to school——'

45

'Not school!' she exclaimed. 'I've run away from all —that.'

'And what does that signify?' he asked swiftly. 'You told me you did the gardening, though it must have been a poor scrap of a garden for you to have dug it. How about a bit of truth now it's daylight and I've fed you—where was this place, and what was it? Some sort of an institution?'

'Yes.' She nodded and wiped her lips, which had a sudden frightened tremor to them. She had known that he would start to probe; that he wouldn't accept the flimsy explanation she had offered him last night. Her fear was that he would demand the name of the institution and guess from that name that she couldn't be the boy she pretended to be. The Virgen de la Soledad was a convent run by nuns for the education of girls, and he would know it!

'An orphanage?' he persisted. 'In Santa Flavia?'

She nodded. 'I—I was there from a baby.'

'You were a foundling, eh?'

'Yes, *señor*. My mother left me there and—and the people who ran it brought me up. Please, do I have to talk about it? I was unhappy there and I meant to run away. You won't—you promised I could stay with you!'

'Of course I promised, and I don't intend to break my word.'

'Oh, you are good!' Impulsively she caught at his right hand and before he could stop her, before she even knew herself what she was going to do, she kissed his fingers.

'My young pup,' he snatched away his hand, and his brows were a single slashing black line above his eyes that seemed to have a stormy sparkle in them, 'you don't have to lick my hand or my boots! I'm not good, you young idiot, I'm bad! I was born into a Castilian

46

family that hides its dirty linen at the bottom of the deepest, darkest chest. But I wouldn't hide mine, and so we were never *simpatico*.'

He got to his feet as he spoke and prowled, panther lean and dark, to the nearest porthole, where he stood broodingly, his profile outlined against the pure light, bronzed and distinct, like that on an old Iberian coin.

'I despise hypocrisy, and pretence.' His voice grated, and Toni's arms crept about a cushion and she hugged it fiercely to her young breasts under the silk of his pyjama jacket. 'The arranged marriage that pretends to be so harmonious, with its undercurrents of jealousy and suspicion. A branch of my mother's family—who were English—had sherry *bodegas* in Jerez, and being a well-off girl she was married off to my father so the two families could be brought together. They hated one another! I was born of hate, *golfo*, not love. I was the issue of a wedding night forced on a girl who feared and hated her Castilian bridegroom. When I was three she ran away with a Cornish artist, who had been roaming through Castile painting its castles. I grew up with a shadowy memory of her; no one ever mentioned her name and I was taught to believe she was dead, until an old nanny let it out in her dotage that *mi madre* was still alive and living in another country. I wanted to get in touch with her, but my father forbade it. From then on he and I were never to be friends, for the old woman told me other things. The terror that dark, grim man had inspired in my English mother. The way she screamed when I was born, and he just looked on with a face like a mask and merely said that it was good the child was a son, to carry on the name and the estates.'

Luque de Mayo broke off, and when he glanced at Toni the dark passion was gone from his features and the mask of irony was back in place.

47

'You're lucky, little ragamuffin,' he said, 'you never had to know whether your mother loved or hated the man who was your father.'

Abruptly he came back to her and eased the cushion out of her clutching hands. 'For heaven's sake, have I frightened you? D'you think I'm going to vent my spleen by kicking you? Let go, and stop clenching your teeth as if getting ready for the blow.' The cushion was jerked away, and the action shifted the neck of the pyjama jacket so that the little heart on its chain came into view against Toni's white skin.

'What have you there?' His fingers reached for it. 'Something you were lucky enough to pinch?'

'Don't!' she knocked his hand away, and her grey-green eyes were hurt. She had known he was going to get at her, if not with a kick, then certainly with a sneer. 'It's mine, and I didn't steal it! I'm not a thief, and if you think I am, then you had better throw me off your boat!'

'You might just go through the porthole.' His hand gripped her slender shoulder. 'What are you doing, you little sissy, with a locket around your neck? Come on, tell me!'

'It's mine,' she said again. 'My mother left it with me.'

'Can you prove that?' His fingers tightened, as if he meant to hurt her physically as he had hurt her mentally.

'Yes——' She fumbled with the locket and sprang the tiny catch. The tiny pictures were revealed, and his eyes narrowed as he examined them. Then he looked directly into Toni's eyes for a long silent moment.

'Want to black my eye, *chico*?' he drawled, and she knew that it would be his only form of apology for disbelieving her when she claimed ownership of the locket.

48

'You've already got a black eye.' She smiled slightly, and that half frightened, half thrilling sensation ran through her as she looked into his eyes that were like sun and shadow ... sun and the flash of gold on a wild hawk's wing. She had only to look at Luque de Mayo to see that a devil and an angel had made him ... an angel who had flown away on unhappy wings when he was still an infant, to go and live with a man who might love her for herself.

'Your mother was a pretty girl, Tonito.' A lean finger snapped shut the locket over the dreamy young face in its frame of fair hair. 'But keep the trinket out of sight—I've enough of a bad reputation without it getting around that I have a pretty boy on board my yacht.'

With an enigmatic expression Luque de Mayo tucked the locket back out of sight under the collar of the pyjama jacket, and Toni tensed at the brush of his fingers and tried not to let it show that her reaction to his touch was quite unboyish, though she had not understood the implication in his words. Into a convent there rarely drifted the rumours and scandals of the wicked world beyond its high and shielding walls.

'Had a good breakfast?' A grin flickered on the edges of her host's ironic lips as he studied her in the pyjama jacket.

'The best, *señor*, thank you. You're a very generous man.'

'Am I?' He quirked a black eyebrow. 'What does it cost me to feed a sprat like you? I do it to amuse myself, as I do most things. It's no virtue on my part to be rich because I had piratical ancestors, men who were a little better at plunder and rapine than they were at more respectable occupations. Do you like money, or the idea of having it?'

'It must be nice to have enough not to go hungry,' she replied, and her eyes dwelt on the stone of the tawny peach which she had recently enjoyed. Somehow the stone symbolised all that might be left of this strange interlude in her life; this voyage to somewhere unknown with a man not really to be known. 'Is your father still alive, *señor*?'

Luque de Mayo shook his dark head. 'He died violently, as he lived. I suppose like everyone else you are impressed by my riches?'

'If you truly hated them and the power they give you, then you'd cast them off, wouldn't you?' she said.

'That, *golfo*, is what they call a kick below the belt.' He reached out and gave her hair a slight tug. 'If I gave up officially what I discard as excess baggage when I travel, then I should be handing over a number of people employed on my estates to the less casual attentions of a cousin of mine who is far more overbearing than I happen to be. I come and I go, and I don't impose rigid rules or play the tyrant. A very capable manager is in charge of things and the arrangement works to our mutual satisfaction. I am the absent master who actually protects by his absence far more than if I cut free altogether—do you understand, Tonito? There are saints who are harsh in their discipline, and sinners who make better masters.'

'Yes——' The memory of those who had controlled her own life was still a vivid one, and Toni's tremor came from that, and from the feel of his fingers on her hair. 'You mean that your cousin is more alike to your father than you are?'

'Indeed he is, *golfo*——' And abruptly Luque de Mayo moved away from her as there came a discreet tap at the door of the state room. '*Adelante!*'

The door opened to admit a sharp-faced little man carrying some garments over his arm. 'The clothes for the boy, *señor*,' he said. 'I was instructed by Captain Martelo to provide them, and he said that if I cut the legs of the trousers about three inches shorter than mine, then they would be a reasonable fit. There is a shirt and a jersey of mine, and a pair of underpants.'

'Ah yes, underpants.' A lazy hand was held out for the things. 'Thank you, steward. These will be most satisfactory for the time being.'

'Very good, *señor*.' The steward cast a sharp look in Toni's direction. 'The captain said that you are not placing the boy directly in my charge—will he be helping with the cabins?'

'In a day or so. We won't press the boy into service just yet, steward. He has had a rough time of it and would be more hindrance than help until he is quite fit. I shall let you know when you can arm him with a polishing rag and a broom.' With a slight gesture towards the door, Luque de Mayo indicated that the steward could depart without further interference in the matter, and Toni breathed a sigh of relief when the door closed behind the short, very efficient-looking figure. She had learned too well at the convent what it was like to be at the mercy of someone who took their duties with religious zeal. Work to them was life itself, and any form of pampering was regarded as a decadent influence on the soul; not to mention the fact that it softened the hands and made them unfit for good honest scrubbing.

'The steward is a good sort, but dedicated to shining brass and carpets that must cringe from the beating he gives them.' Luque de Mayo gave his sardonic smile as he tipped Toni's chin with a lean finger. 'I shouldn't be scared of him, Tonito. I am the boss of this yacht.'

'The crew won't like me,' she said. 'They'll think you are pampering me—perhaps I should start doing some work——?'

'You will take a holiday from work, and that is an order.'

'Is it, *señor*?' A marvellous order that bore no relation to those she was accustomed to taking. '*Gracias, señor.*'

'Being impudent, are you? Here, take these to your cabin and get dressed in your own time. I am going up on the bridge for a chat with Martelo. Catch!'

Toni caught the garments, which smelled of soap and the fresh sea air in which they had dried. There was no smell of earth and stale tobacco smoke on these, and she was halfway in her cabin when Luque de Mayo said drawlingly:

'Don't put the underpants on back to front.'

Inside her cabin Toni leaned against the door, clutching the garments to her until her heartbeats slowed down again. Had he guessed? Did he know that she was a girl? Was he aiding and abetting the imposture for devious reasons of his own?

Toni couldn't tell ... she couldn't really be sure. Luque de Mayo was far too subtle and complex for a convent girl to fathom.

CHAPTER FOUR

WITHIN a few days the bruise on Toni's temple had lost its dramatic look and faded to a violet mark against her skin. She soon discovered that she loved being up on the deck where the sea breezes seemed to blow through her mind even as they ruffled her hair. She had longed for freedom, but never in her wildest dreams had she imagined that it would come like this, on a stranger's yacht.

She would lean for hours against the yacht rails and watch the proud white bows slicing through the water, cutting it away like yards of blue silk. The graceful bows were painted magnolia white except for a scarlet line just below the gleaming rails.

Toni had no idea that she cut rather a colourful figure herself, clad in the shortened jeans and wearing over them a sailor shirt. Her red hair was stroked by the sunlight, and the sea light had got into her eyes as she stood there drinking it all in. So many miles of blue and buoyant water, which looked in this halcyon mood as if it had never known a storm, and could never know one.

It didn't occur to Toni that she was a natural sailor until Luque de Mayo remarked on the fact.

'Perhaps the sea is in your blood,' he drawled, an arm resting upon the rail as he smoked a cheroot, clad himself in close-cut white trousers and a tawny shirt that made him extra fascinating in Toni's eyes. He seemed so supple and lazily unpredictable; alert even when at ease, not to be closely approached even when he came within inches of touching her.

'I never imagined that the sea could be so beautiful, *señor*. It goes on and on, until it seems to join itself to heaven.'

'So, Tonito, the sea and the sky appear to you as lovers. I've always regarded the moon as the mistress of the sea, but you have yet to see the moon riding the waves at night. How many new things there are for you to witness? How much you have to learn about life. I almost envy your innocence, do you know that?'

Toni cast him a look and smiled impishly.

'What are you thinking, you pup, that I have never been as innocent as you?'

'I'm sure you never could have been, *señor*. You— well, you never had my background, did you?'

'You believe that the devil only finds fun for idle hands, eh?'

'I don't think he's very interested in those whose hands are either plunged into greasy water or busy with a scrubbing brush.'

'All the same, Tonito, he whispered to you that you might run away from your greasy pots and your scrubbing brush, and fall in with one of his disciples. Nothing happens quite by chance, so my Latin blood tells me, and just as I was feeling a black ennui, fate drops you into my hands. What if I ruin you, *chico*, eh? What if the devil in me decides to corrupt that miraculous innocence of yours?'

Toni's slim hands gripped the rail when he said that, and she saw the brooding, faintly devilish expression on his face. Again she wondered if he knew that she was really a girl ... and then as she felt the sea wind in her face and breathed the aroma of his cheroot, she knew that she would rather be rended body and limb by him than ever have to go back to the convent, to face all that stern chastity and unrelenting humility of body and spirit.

'I don't care,' she said recklessly. 'Do what you like with me, *señor*. I just—just don't want to be sent away from you. I'd rather stay with you than anyone——'

'So the devil you don't know is preferable in your eyes to the one you do know?'

'Yes.' She said it firmly. 'Anyway, I don't think you're as bad as you make out. Saints can be terribly harsh and I—I'd sooner be with you. You make me feel alive——'

'You mean I keep you on edge, like electricity,' he drawled. 'You and I, *golfo*, are at the stage when we are intrigued by each other. We are the opposite sides of a coin ... you have nothing but your unblemished youth, and I have everything but youth without a stain on it. I excite your curiosity, and you excite mine, and I promise that for as long as this cruise lasts you'll stay with me, but when it ends—well, I can't make any promise when that happens, Tonito. We'll leave it with fate, shall we?'

'All right,' she said, and swore to herself that she wouldn't think about the end of the voyage but would enjoy every moment while it lasted.

There were evenings during those halcyon days when Luque de Mayo and his captain dined on deck under the dense massses of stars. Toni was not invited to the table and was content to sit alone with her plate of food in a secluded corner of the deck; she was the cabin-boy, and the *señor* made no comment, he merely looked and quirked an eyebrow the first time she curled down against the rail and ate alone, neither of the crew, nor acceptable as a guest. It was the way she wanted it; she could never have felt at ease with the stern eyes of Captain Martelo upon her. To him she was a waif and stray who had no business on board the

Miranda, and for the most part he ignored her.

For those evening meals Luque de Mayo always dressed formally in a crisp white jacket over perfectly cut dark trousers, and his bow tie was either of maroon or midnight silk against the speckless white of his shirt-front. The captain wore his smart tropical uniform, and from her corner Toni would study the two men and think how different they were, and yet how distinctive in their Latin darkness of skin and hair. Their deep voices would drift to her as they discussed matters relating to the yacht and the possible vagaries of the weather.

Toni, with her plate balanced on her updrawn knees, ate her *cazuela de ave* and enjoyed every mouthful of the spicy mixture of vegetables and corn. Whenever Luque de Mayo laughed in that deep, short way of his, it came like music to her ears. She often felt that for a man who had so much, he had had little of real happiness. She sometimes wondered if he had ever loved anyone ... a woman of the world, who dressed in silk and painted her lips and her eyes. Sister Imaculata had called such women creatures of sin, who lived only for pleasure and the pampering of their bodies. They scented their skin, and they knew exactly how to make men fall madly in love with them.

Yes, she decided, Luque de Mayo had known such women. How could they resist such a man as he, who had wealth and distinction, and the charisma of an unusual personality? But love ... had love eluded him and made him cynical?

'I refuse to believe that the kind of weather we've been enjoying can undergo a sudden change,' Toni heard him say, in that lazily grating voice of his. 'Anyway, how can you be so sure, Martelo? Are you in commune with the stars or something?'

'In communication by radio with the people at

56

Mawgan Plas,' the captain rejoined. 'Whenever we set sail, *señor*, you refuse to acknowledge the presence of the radio, but the seas have been running high in the bay for several days, and we are heading that way, are we not?'

'It's time I paid a visit,' said Luque de Mayo. 'If we are running into a storm, then it won't be the first time, and I'm not worried about the *Miranda*. She's the only female in my life that I'd ever trust. She's as sound as a bell—and there's nothing on board to jinx us, is there?'

A short silence followed his words, and glancing across at him from the shadows where she sat, his lean figure illumined by the rigging lanterns, Toni saw him twirl the wine in his stemmed glass. 'What's on your mind, Martelo?' he asked lazily. 'I suspect there is something—is it the young Tonito? Do you imagine he might have brought a dash of bad luck on board with him? Poor stray pup, I'd hate to tie that can to his tail.'

The captain shot a frowning look in Toni's direction, and she tautened and was made nervous by his dark and searching eyes. She had heard of the superstition among sailors relating to the bad luck of having a female on board a ship. But they thought her a boy ... didn't they? It was a relief when the two men began to discuss the virtues of the *Miranda*.

'The only female a man might love without having to endure tears and tantrums, or any other of the torments associated with a woman.' Luque de Mayo tossed back his wine in a gesture of total cynicism. 'I am sure you agree with me, Martelo, as you have never succumbed to the perils of matrimony.'

'When I was a young man I never had enough money for the girl of my village whom I really wanted,' the captain replied. 'By the time I was well-off enough to have her, she had been married to a pig farmer and had several piglets of her own.'

Luque de Mayo gave his short laugh, that seemed to end even as it begun. 'If she'd had the nerve to defy parental convention she could have had you, and I'm sure you smell much better than a pig farmer. Perhaps it's for the best, Martelo. Marriage is too often hell, and rarely a heaven on earth.'

'Do you suppose, *señor*, that it was meant to be a heaven?' The captain spoke drily as he drank his wine. 'Surely that would be placing a great strain on the man and the woman. Why, the woman would have to be a veritable angel in order to provide such a sanctuary for a man.'

'Quite so, and that is why it's more comfortable to remain solo, eh?' Luque de Mayo leaned back in his seat and turned his face to the stars. He studied them for a long silent moment, and then quite distinctly Toni heard him sigh. 'Yes, Martelo, marriage is for the young whose illusions are intact, and for the elderly who fear loneliness.'

'It sounds a likely philosophy, *señor*, but in your case you are duty bound to marry while you are still a comparatively young man.' A stern note had crept into the captain's voice, almost as if he reproved a seaman who wouldn't obey orders. 'You have property and so you must have a son to inherit. Your course is a clear one——'

'Ah, but not a settled one.' The lean hands broke a bread roll with a crisp sound, as if those hands would break the chains of family duty if they could. 'The very idea of marrying just to get a son is a course I find hard to take. If I were entirely Spanish—perhaps.' His shoulders lifted the smooth whiteness of his dinner jacket in a cynical shrug. 'In me, Martelo, is mixed two wines— the warm red wine of the south, and the cool dry wine of the north. Even as I become intoxicated, I become cold stone sober again. The Latin in me reaches out for the red carnation in the rich black hair, but the Anglo-Saxon in me provides a puzzle to which I have not yet found the answer. What that side of me wants I have not yet found out—it may be everything, or it may be nothing. Like Janus I look both ways at once and I find it impossible to steer a straight course through life—as you do, *amigo*.'

He laughed shortly, this time with a touch of harshness. 'What if I married and made life a hell for the woman? It's in me to do it—in my blood, Martelo.'

These words came almost like a whisper, as a whip strikes, as a snake stings, and Toni gave a shiver when they reached her. Was that why he thrust love away from him and took in its place the passing pleasures of the moment? Did he fear that heredity would prove too strong and that like his father he would prove a terrible husband?

'We are what we are meant to be,' he drawled, 'and that, Martelo, is why you are a captain and I am a rake.'

The captain didn't contradict the statement, Toni noticed. He sailed the *Miranda* for Luque de Mayo and probably knew him as well as anyone was permitted to know him, yet Toni wanted to fly to his defence. She wanted to say that he took people for better or worse, without judgement or prejudice, and that in itself was a virtue. Though born an *hidalgo* he had by some personal magic escaped being haughty and snobbish.

Toni gazed across at him, almost unseen in her shadows so that it was comparatively safe to adore that lean face in the glimmers of lantern light and star glow. Even if she did see sin in that face, she also saw a humorous hint of tenderness—he might kill a man,

59

but he might also die to save a dog, and Toni loved him as she had never been able to love those stern saints who had ruled her life for seventeen years.

'What's the matter, Tonito?' Suddenly Luque de Mayo was looking directly across at her. 'I can see your eyes from here, big as silver kettles. Look at the young pup, Martelo. I could kick him and he'd lick my hand —*por dios,* you don't find that kind of devotion every day of the week! It almost warms my cynical and sinful heart to be thought so much of.'

It hurt Toni that he should mock her, yet she knew that he would always do it. It was his shield and his mace, to deride those who cared for him, for like his mother when he was a boy, they might care one day and be gone the next.

'If you kicked me, I'd kick back,' she rejoined. 'I'm not that soft!'

'You are impudent, *jovencito,*' it was Captain Martelo who spoke, 'when the *señor* is good enough to feed you and take you in off the streets. We run a ship, not a home for waifs and strays, so you mind your manners when you talk to the——'

'I didn't ask to be brought here!' Toni jumped to her feet. 'I didn't ask for anything that happened to me after I was knocked out—I hate charity! It's all I've ever had!' She rushed away, heading blindly for the iron stairs that led below. She ran as a female runs from the only man who can ever deeply hurt her. Pup ... ragamuffin ... something to be stroked or mocked as the mood took him. Alone in the darkness she fought the pain of being almost nothing to him, beyond an amusement that might pass as quickly as it had come. It was something she had to learn to live with, for it was all she was going to have.

Half an hour later when he came to his state room, Toni was standing by the porthole, quiet and subdued

60

as she had learned to be at the convent when a reprimand was due. She had been impudent and that was like snapping the hand that fed her ... but it wasn't the impudence he would mind so much as the braggadocio. No one kicked Luque de Mayo, least of all a waif in cut-down trousers.

The light flicked on and Toni blinked against the sudden brightness, and tensed where she stood.

'Why are you standing there like a stick?' His eyes played over her, oddly glinting in that way they had, so that it was impossible to guess his thoughts or to read his intentions. 'Are you waiting for me to take a stick to you—is it what you're used to, *golfo*? A whipping whenever you forget your place?'

'It isn't my place to be rude to you, *señor*.' Toni spoke gruffly because her throat ached from the tears she had learned to hold back. 'You've been good to me—better than anyone because you haven't preached. If you want to kick me, then I shan't mind.'

'Is that a fact?' He took her by the shoulder and gave her a look that was as cruel as any kick would have been. 'Are you a soft young fool, then? You wouldn't put up a fight if I took a fit to bully you?'

'You just about own me, don't you, *señor*? It's up to you what you do with me.'

'Don't be so infernally humble!' The lean hand shook her and she gritted her teeth because he jarred the slight bones of her shoulder. 'I like a proud young pup with a bit of spirit in him, not a hang-jaw cur who asks for the boot. I saw too much of that when I was a boy, animals and people scared out of their wits by a mere man because he carried a whip and had a bit of authority. To hell with it, Tonito, you'll not cringe when I look it you, or touch you! What's that look for? Why are you flinching?'

'You—you're sort of hurting me, *señor*.' She spoke in

a half-stifled voice, for in his momentary passion, over-
come by memories of a boyhood he would always hate,
he had literally ground his hard fingers into Toni's
shoulder and the pain had been sickening.

'*Dios!*' He let go of her and stared down at her face,
which had lost every vestige of colour. 'I never meant
to almost break your bones, *golfo*. I wouldn't hurt you
on purpose—here, let me see what damage I've caused!'

Swiftly, adroitly, before she could pull away, his lean
fingers undid the buttons of her shirt and he exposed
her shoulder before she could stop him. She shivered
from head to toe as Luque de Mayo ran his fingers
over the place where he had left an impression against
the whiteness of her skin.

'*Por dios,* what are you made of, Tonito, to mark like
that? You're just skin and bone and nerve, aren't you?
Stop shivering, there's a good *chico*. It wasn't my intention to hurt you—come, you do believe me, don't you?'

'Yes, *señor*,' but she couldn't control the tremors, and
with an oath he lifted her and settled her on the divan.
He went to the drinks cabinet and took from it a bottle
of tawny liquid; the bottle itself was an odd shape with
big dimples in the glass.

'A tot of whisky will settle those nerves of yours,
Tonito. In all frankness I don't know what I'm going
to do with you—I'm not good for you. Young things
are not my forte——'

'No, it's me!' She sat up sharply, for nothing was
more alarming than the faintest hint that he would
rid himself of the pup who had feelings to hurt and
bones to bruise. 'I'm stupid and terribly backward, but
I'll try to be sensible and not behave like a kid—only
don't send me away! I couldn't bear that—I think I'd
want to jump overboard——'

'You do that, *golfo*, and there will be hell to pay.

Drink this and stop being a little fool—drink it, I said, not spill it!'

'Th-thank you.' Toni's teeth knocked against the rim of the glass, and she shuddered at the strong taste. 'Ugh!'

'That's a delightful reaction, I must say.' Luque de Mayo lounged against the table and drank his own whisky with obvious enjoyment. 'You aren't stupid, Tonito, you're just too sensitive for your own good. How on earth do I deal with that when I'm a swine myself, with about as much heart as a piece of *chonta* wood?'

'I—I think you have a heart, *señor*,' she said swiftly. 'More heart than most people—those who pretend to be so good and spend all their time meting out punishments. I think it's the good people who have clock-work hearts.'

'Do you?' He laughed shortly. 'You're a funny sort of sprat to have landed in my net, with a kind of half-baked philosophy that hits closer to the mark than it ought, for a kid of your age. In the right hands, and handled with care, you might turn out to be quite an intelligent and charming creature—but my hands aren't the right ones, Tonito. They've dipped into the devil's work more often than they should have done, and I don't want to ruin you——'

'You couldn't,' she said passionately. 'You could never do that!'

'Of course I could.' His face was wholly sardonic in that moment; a lean, dark mask almost sinister in its self-knowing. 'You're at my mercy and I could do what I liked with you, and you'd probably end up skulking some shady dock for those you could corrupt with tricks learned from me. Young things like you can be taught all manner of tricks, and I don't doubt that I'd enjoy being your tutor—only each time I thought of those big innocent eyes of yours, I'd burn in hell a lot sooner than my allotted time.'

'I—I don't care what you do with me,' she muttered, staring into the glass that still held most of the whisky he had given her. 'It would be hell for me if you sent me away to people I don't know, to whom I'd be just another charity child.'

'That's the stinger, is it, *golfo*? The charity part? Having to take from other people?'

'You're different,' she said fiercely. 'You don't make it seem like charity——'

'No, I make it seem like fun,' he said drily. 'Left-off clothes from my steward, a plate of food in a corner of my deck, a bruised shoulder you didn't ask for. I'm a delightful guardian——'

'The only one I want!' Her enormous eyes clung to his face, while the left-off shirt still lay open against her thin shoulder, where the skin was now dark from that punishing grip of his. 'If you knew what my life has been——'

'I think I can guess, Tonito, but you could never know what my life has been. You would be the devil's apprentice if you stayed with me—is that what you want?'

'I don't want anything else, *señor*.'

'Don't be a young fool! You're too young to know what you want, or what is good for you.' Luque de Mayo strode with sudden impatience to the nearest porthole, where he stood gazing out at the star-drenched sea, his profile outlined in all its pagan chiselling against the backdrop of milky light. 'I'm not good for an impressionable young thing like you, my waif of the night. But—I don't know—I wonder if you'll be good for me? Do you think you might?'

'I'd do anything for you, *señor*——' Toni knelt up on the divan, so eager to please him that she would have scrubbed the *Miranda* from stem to stern if he had asked her to do so.

'I believe you would, at that.' He turned moodily from the porthole and studied her with narrowed eyes that flickered strangely behind his lowered lashes. 'For the life of me I can't think what I've done to deserve you—you make it damned hard for me to do the right thing, *golfo*, and as usual I'm going to do the wrong thing——'

'You're not going to send me away to other people?' Toni cried out, fervently. 'I can see that you're not, *señor*. You're smiling!'

'It's the devil's smile, you little fool. Don't you know that? It means that instead of resisting temptation, I am falling from grace once again. The serpent whispers and I lend an ear. The apple falls and I pick it up. It's a rather green apple, at present, but it has distinct possibilities.'

'I'll work hard, *señor*,' Toni promised. 'I'll earn my keep and I won't be any bother——'

'Work?' Luque de Mayo snapped his fingers. 'What sort of work could a young scarecrow like you do for me? I have all the servants I require. You, *golfo*, can be my page, my young squire, and we'll polish you up, and fatten you somewhat, and rig you out. You can go to damnation with me, if it's what you want so badly.'

Toni gave a happy sigh and nodded. And just to prove that she was all set to go to the devil with him, she gulped down the remainder of her whisky—and very nearly choked herself.

Luque de Mayo was thumping some breath back into her when there was a knock on the door and Captain Martelo came to tell him that the storm that was blowing in the bay to which they were heading was directly in their path and they would run into it in about an hour's time.

'Will it be a bad one, Martelo?' Luque de Mayo stood there, almost negligently, a hand at rest in his pocket and that flame that betokened excitement flickering in his eyes.

'It could well be, *señor*. I've ordered those boxes of cargo to be well lashed——'

'Ah, so you're expecting quite a blow, and that cargo is rather a precious one. Equipment for the hospital, Martelo. Having endowed the place I thought I should go a step further and see that it had all the latest in drugs and instruments. An hour, eh?' He shot a look at Toni, who still looked rather fraught after her choking session. 'Afraid of storms, *chico*?' he asked.

'I've never been in a storm at sea, *señor*,' she replied. 'I'll try not to be too alarmed.'

Luque de Mayo smiled briefly. 'Hop off to your berth, Tonito, and get an hour's sleep. When the storm hits us it will be too noisy for sleeping, for there is nothing more thunderous than the angry ocean, spitting and snarling it out with the winds and the lightning. I'll come with you, Martelo, and do my bit to see that everything is secured.'

The two men went away, their voices and footsteps fading along the companionway to the stairs. Toni wandered into her own cubbyhole and sat down on the bed. The whisky had made her feel drowsy and she let her head fall back against the pillow and she drifted pleasantly on the edge of sleep. The coming storm didn't frighten her ... she felt that nothing could ever do that while Luque de Mayo was within calling distance. What she had feared had passed ... he had promised to let her stay with him, and she didn't care what the future held so long as it held him. Deprived all her life of someone to love, she now loved for the first time, and possibly realised the irony of a convent girl loving the devil.

The storm when it hit them was a thing of fury that seemed to last for hours. Great gouts of water flung themselves at the yacht, and the lightning was fierce and silvery, edged by alternate streaks of flaming red and blue. The *Miranda* was rocked back and forth like a toy boat in a bath, the high waves sweeping over her decks and soaking the lashed sails.

The lightning lit the sea, and from the porthole where she crouched Toni could see how enormous were the waves, like mountains that might fall upon the yacht and crush it to matchwood. It was terrifying and yet it was stimulating, and when in the midst of it Luque de Mayo came to join her at the porthole it became thrilling.

'So you don't tremble at storms,' he murmured, as he ran light fingers across her shoulders.

'No,' she shook her head. 'I only tremble at one thing, *señor*, being cast off by you.'

'Little fool,' he growled. 'The day might come when you'll regret ever meeting me, and you'll call yourself worse than a fool.'

'I'll never have any regrets about meeting you, *señor*.' She turned her head to look at him and her eyes were wide and steady, unflinching as the lightning blazed, flame-tinged.

He stared down at her pale triangular face, unmasked by the lightning, and then in shadow again.

'Don't tempt the gods with statements like that, Tonito. Never be sure of anything, for fate has a way of showing us that nothing in this life is ever certain or for ever. Those waves out there are powerful enough to lift this yacht on her face and send us all to the bottom of the sea ... we are, quite absolutely, in the hands of fate. We might live to see the morning sun shining on the banks of Mawgan Plas, or we might drown. Doesn't that prospect make you tremble?'

'I'm not afraid when I'm with you, *señor*,' she said simply.

'*Dios*, there you go again making rash statements! Why do you make them—do you believe that the devil takes care of his own?'

She smiled a little, and couldn't tell him that to die with him would be more like living than to have to live without him. 'Perhaps I do believe that,' she said. 'Don't you?'

'You young scamp!' He gave her a mocking swipe that stopped short of actual contact with her face. 'Feeling your oats because I've made rash promises about keeping you with me?' Their eyes clung in the glare of the lightning. 'If we ride out the storm, then we put into the bay tomorrow. Heaven knows what the people there are going to make of you, *golfo*. They might take you for my by-blow—will you mind that?'

She shook her head. 'It's what I am, *señor*.'

'Some people may be unkind, Tonito.'

'I'm used to that—I don't think it's in people to be kind to those who are nothing, and have nothing, and you're the only one——'

'Shut up, or you'll turn my head.' Luque de Mayo laid a finger against her lips. 'I can't put you to work in my kitchen or my garden—you do understand that?'

'I'm in your hands, *señor*,' she said. 'I leave it up to you what you do with me.'

'Then so be it!' He looked above her head, into the raw blaze of the lightning as it lit the rain-lashed night. 'You're in my hands, Tonito, for better or worse!'

And it was then, as if his almost reckless words were a challenge flung in the face of destiny, the yacht gave an awful lurch and what had been a slightly pitching floor became a sudden slide down which Toni was falling into darkness and noise. As she was flung forward she heard a combination of sounds that blended

68

into a single shocking sound as glass shattered, as wood splintered and metal tore loose from the body of the vessel and spilled the life of the *Miranda* into the heaving seas.

Toni lay stunned where she had fallen, and as that first tumult of noise subsided, there came the bursting whine of distress rockets, and she added her voice to them by crying out: *'Señor!'*

Hands clutched at her in the darkness and there was a crackle of broken glass underfoot as hoisting her up with him, a savage mixture of Spanish and English on his lips, he used all his strength and his agility to get both of them out of the cabin that was filling rapidly with water. The only reality, the one sensation that was not part of the nightmare, was the painful grip of Luque's hands holding on to her as the incoming sea washed hungrily about her legs, pulling her downward even as he pulled her out on the frightening slope of the deck.

By then they were both on their knees, clinging together as they were pitched forward, through the deck hatch which hung open above the black pit of the sea.

They fell endlessly into the high-flung waves, and the lightning flared as they struck the water. *'Señor...'* It was like the last cry of the doomed.

'Niña ... I have you!' It was like the last laugh of the damned.

The ocean whirled them in its stormy embrace, and as the water flung itself over her head and her breath was snatched from her by the relentless sweep of the waves, she knew with her last bit of awareness that he had never been fooled.

Niña ... the Spanish word for girl.

CHAPTER FIVE

THE nurse gazed curiously at the girl in the hospital bed, her pallor intensified by the sea light that quivered on the walls and ceiling of the room.

The girl didn't look as if she belonged to anyone, let alone that distinctive man of the world who sat in Matron's office right now, talking casually about his bride-to-be.

Antonia Fleet, who had been with him on his yacht when it had sunk off the bay of Mawgan Plas, grinding into the rock that lay jagged beneath the sea, dangerous in smooth weather and all the more so when a storm struck the Cornish coast. The yacht now lay in battered pieces under the white spume that washed endlessly over the rocks; no more would she proudly sail the seas, her pennant waving in the wind above her decks so that the scarlet salamander seemed alive against the canvas.

Toni woke with a little moan out of the frightening dream of lashing waves and thunder that cracked the skies, and she opened her eyes with a sense of shock. It still seemed incredible that she could see and feel and take nourishment. It still seemed impossible that she had survived the storm and the sinking of the *Miranda*.

'Awake, are you, dear?' A blue and white figure came to the bedside and Toni gazed wordlessly at the cheerful face bent to her. 'Come along, sit up and let me comb your hair. You have a visitor and you don't want to keep him waiting.'

A visitor? Toni struggled into a sitting position and allowed the nurse to run a comb through her short hair. She looked very young and slight in her white nightdress, so that her hair seemed like jags of flame against her pale cheeks.

'There, you don't look too bad. You're not really damaged, just exhausted and in need of a few days' rest——'

'How long have I been here?' Toni clutched at the nurse's hand. 'Where am I?'

'In a nice private room of St. Mawgan's very own, very new hospital.' The nurse patted the thin fingers consolingly. 'You're still shaken up after what you've been through—nearly getting drowned like that! Just a bit of a girl not long out of the schoolroom, I shouldn't wonder, and in need of a bit of mothering. These Spaniards! They don't believe in waiting, do they?'

Toni's heart gave a wild throb and her eyes seemed to enlarge as she stared at the nurse. 'Is it him? Has he come to see me? Oh, how marvellous that he wasn't drowned!'

'I don't imagine that you drown his sort very easily.' The nurse spoke drily, having seen too much of the many sides of people to have many illusions left. This hospital existed because of that tall, half-foreign personage, but that didn't alter the fact that he had a sort of arrogant lordliness that made all his actions seem suspect in the eyes of the duty-bound and the rather self-righteous. He had more money, and more self-willed, sardonic charm than was good for anyone, and it had to be his idea of a jest, putting it around that he meant to marry someone as young and unsophisticated as this girl. It was true she had been with him on his yacht, but somehow she didn't look the usual pleasure-seeking female he went around with. Nor was she some common little piece who had bewitched him ... no, there was nothing like that about the girl.

'No.' A slight smile lit Toni's eyes. 'The devil takes care of his own—those waves were so enormous and you just couldn't catch your breath. They just kept snatching it away——'

And once again her breath was snatched away as the door of the room was suddenly swept open and Luque de Mayo walked in as if he owned the place. 'You can go, nurse,' he said. 'Your Matron tells me that Miss Fleet is well on the mend and ready for a visitor. What do you say, Toni? Want to see me?'

His eyes met hers, flickering gold and black in the lean face that was devilish and wonderful at one and the same time. Toni flung out a hand to him, wordlessly, and he caught it in his steely grip.

'Don't overtire the young lady, my lord.' The nurse spoke with prim severity and rustled her way from the room, and all the time Luque had a wicked quirk to his mouth.

'A bit of a tartar, eh? She bosses you about, *picara*?'

'She means well—and she called you a lord?' Toni gazed up at him with the bemused eyes of a child who had been lost and was now found.

'Lord Luque of Hades,' he said drily, and sat down in the chair beside her bed. He wore a car-coat in smooth tweed, with an astrakhan collar, and he looked lazily distinguished, and to Toni's slight dismay less the Spaniard with whom she had sailed and more the English gentleman.

'Well, how are you feeling?' He leaned forward and placed a thumb against her temple, under the flick of auburn hair, smoothing her fine skin that showed the blue veins so distinctly. 'You still look as fragile as a piece of bone china, but I'm assured that you are fit in wind and limb and can be released from these clinical environs at the end of the week. Will you like that?'

'Oh yes,' she said, feeling his light touch like a bene-
diction, bringing her alive after all those hours of feeling so numb and so alone. Her eyes searched his ...
what was he going to do with her? They were in England now, where it would be circumspect for a man in
his position to cut himself loose from the embarrassing
orphan who had gone about on his yacht in chopped-
down jeans and a blue sailor jersey. She couldn't do
that now ... she couldn't be with him as she had been
on board the *Miranda*.

'Are you going to send me to school ... something
like that?' she asked, and a little hint of mutiny settled
about her lips. 'I won't go, *señor*. I'd sooner get myself
a job.'

'What sort of a job?' he drawled. 'Doing what ...
washing dishes in a café?'

'You're horribly cruel when you like,' she retorted,
jerking her head away from his touch, which a moment
ago had been so welcome.

'Horrible enough to marry, or are you still masquer-
ading as a boy? Outlandishly liberated as this land has
become, I don't think impolite society would quite
approve of a lordship taking a lad to the altar.'

'Now you're being sarcastic,' she muttered, and then
gave a gasp as the taut power of his arm encircled her
slight waist and he caught her to him, holding her so
that she felt weak and frightened.

'You impudent little cuss, I should have let you
drown and then I'd be shot of you. A man with a bit
more sense would send you packing, but I never was
the sort who subscribed to convention and the easy
path. You may not remember, but just before the
Miranda ran on the rocks, you placed yourself in my
hands and I accepted you, for better or worse. That
acceptance might as well stand. You might as well

73

marry me.'

Of all the shattering things which had happened since Toni had found herself in Luque's cabin, this proposal of marriage was the most heart-shaking. Every scrap of strength seemed to leave her and she collapsed against his shoulder and clung there, afraid to believe that she might have a permanent place in his life. It just wasn't possible ... Luque couldn't marry a girl who had been placed as a foundling in a convent, and who had run away because she hadn't the courage to become a nun. It seemed as ludicrous to imagine herself the bride of Luque as it had been to imagine herself a bride of the church.

'Are you so bored by my proposal that you've decided to take a nap?' He took her pointed chin in his fingers and forced her to look at him. He searched her face from which every trace of colour had vanished, and looked deep into her unbelieving eyes.

'Well, it's done all the time in Spain,' he said, and his eyes gleamed oddly. 'Love doesn't come into it. Love won't, for you're only seventeen, and I might as well take care of you and see that you don't spend your life up to your elbows in greasy water. Besides, there's a saying in Spain that if you save a life, then it belongs to you.'

'But you don't have to marry me,' she said faintly. 'I could work for you—I could be a maid in your house.'

'You can stop being so blasted humble!' He gave her a shake. 'Anyway, think how the tongues would wag. The cat's well out of the bag that you were on the *Miranda*, and I've already told everyone that we are going to be married. Like it or not, *golfo*, you are very much the fiancée of Luque de Mayo, and as such you had better be branded and ringed.'

The brand was the pressure of his lips against her cheek, and she just couldn't stop shaking as he held

74

her hand and slid a ring on to the third finger. The band was of gold set with a star-shaped diamond that sparkled like a tropic dawn, with deep in the heart of it a blue flame, glowing and alive, pure as true virtue.

Toni stared into the heart of the diamond as if she were mesmerised. The girls at the convent had talked about rings and romance, but such things had seemed as distant from Toni's life as the stars themselves. She could see the dazzle of the stone, and she could feel the weight of it against the bone and flesh of her hand, but instead of delight she felt a sense of absurdity.

Such rings were meant for the beautiful, and the adored, and she was neither of these impossible things. She was a runaway, a gamine with her hair chopped off to subdue its redness.

Great tears filled her eyes and she slowly shook her head as she gazed at the ring, the diamond shimmering as a tear broke on her lashes and fell down her face. 'A man like you—you have to marry someone very beautiful, who makes you feel—not as you feel about me. You're sorry for me, *señor*.'

'Am I?' He tilted her face again and regarded her tears with a quizzical expression. 'Is that such a bad thing for a man like me, who has led his life, shaped his ends to suit himself? Why shouldn't I marry you? You're a female——'

'You knew all along,' she muttered, and her lashes felt wet and heavy as she tried to avoid his eyes. 'You let me make an ass of myself in trousers with the legs chopped down—is that why you want to—to marry me, so you can have fun at my expense?'

'What a suspicious little cuss you are!' He gave his brief and cynical laugh and wiped a tear from her cheek with his thumb. 'I've not seen a woman cry for thirty years, and that's quite a time, eh? I was a mere boy when I found my mother weeping her heart out in a Moorish loggia of the house in which we lived, which was never like a real home. She was weeping because she was going to run away with her lover, but I didn't know that—until she had gone. I never saw her again, but when she died she left me the house in which she had found real happiness with her Cornishman, who himself died in a storm while out fishing. That is why I come to Mawgan Plas each year, to keep a rendezvous with the memory of my mother. Mawgan Plas is now a lonely house and it needs a woman there—someone who has never known a real home and will, perhaps, love it.'

Toni gazed at him wordlessly, feeling as if he had clenched those lean fingers around her heart. Dare she believe that he meant what he said? That he wished to marry her for the sake of his mother's house, so that when he went again on one of his restless rambles, someone would be there to take care of things, and keep warm its rooms with the love that only the homeless could give.

'It would be lovely for me, just to look after the house,' she said softly. 'There's no need to marry me——'

'To the devil with it, girl!' Suddenly his face had a dark danger to it. 'Marrying you will keep me safe from making some kind of hell for myself. It's in my blood. I'm capable of it. You, Toni, will be the sword of chastity between me and the devils in my nature. Come, doesn't that sort of arrangement appeal to you? Man and wife in name only?'

'In name only?' she echoed after him. 'You mean——?'

'Yes, that is what I mean. You need a keeper, and in a sense you already belong to me. If you were ten years younger I could adopt you, but a year from now you'll be a woman, and the safest bet all round is a

76

mariage de convenance.'

'Are you very sure, *señor?*' Her tears had dried, but a most curious pain had hold of her heart. He asked her to marry him, but he didn't want her for a real wife. He didn't love her in that way at all.

'I'm sure, Toni, but we do have to get straight between us exactly where you came from—now don't pull away like that, as if I've slung a halter around your neck. Whoever those people were, they were your guardians and I have to get their permission for the marriage. They will have your birth certificate——'

'They won't, *señor.*' She tilted her chin. 'I was abandoned on the *torno,* the foundling wheel, of a convent of Santa Flavia. All I had in the world was a locket around my neck, but no papers, no indication of where I came from. I was just left, and I was one of those who was going to be a novice.'

'A nun?' he exclaimed. 'You, Toni?'

'Yes.' She bit her lip at his obvious amusement. 'I know it sounds funny, but it happens to be true. That's why I ran away. I couldn't face such a life—one has to be so—so good, and I have a temper, and such a lot of imagination. I kept thinking of the world beyond the convent walls, and so one afternoon I stole some clothes from the gardening boy and I climbed over the wall and got away. You took me for a gipsy pickpocket, and all the time I was quite honest if I was nothing else.'

'So, little nun who never was, I need ask no one for your hand. Better to steer clear of the good Sisters, for they might want you back——'

'Oh no, Luque, I couldn't endure that!' Suddenly she clung to him like a young animal in distress, burying her face against the astrakhan collar of his coat, breathing his cheroot smoke, and loving him with a wild mixture of innocence and worship. 'I don't want to be a nun!'

'You shan't be, so stop shaking like a young aspen.'

'I'll be anything but that—always behind high walls, always so good that you have to punish others to make them good—like the Spanish Inquisition.'

'How you do go on, *golfo*!' He rocked her in his arms as if she were a child. 'Shut up, now, before you catch hysteria and I have to answer to the blue and white dragon for upsetting you. You don't have to be anything but mine. You'll leave this place at the end of the week, and in the meantime I shall make the necessary arrangements for our nuptials. They might as well take place at the Church of the Lilies near Mawgan Plas, where my mother and her man are buried. You aren't so superstitious that you won't like that, *niña*?'

Niña ... he had called her that when he had saved her life, and by using that lovely Spanish term right now he made it possible for Toni to accept his proposal and his plans.

'It sounds a lovely church, *señor*.'

'It is, and our union there is going to set the tongues wagging. The Cornish folk are inclined to dwell on the past, when we Spaniards raided them and carried off their girls in our galleons. It still rankles, and in their eyes I resemble those dark marauders and I have their ravishing ways. There will be some shaking of heads and dire predictions when you and I emerge from the church with its blessings on my black head, and your very young one.'

As he said this he studied her very intently, his eyes searching out all the youth and innate courage in her face with its high shadowed cheekbones, vulnerable lips and grey eyes haunted by tints of green.

'Yes, they'll pass judgment on the two of us,' he drawled. 'Satan and the seraph.'

'Please—don't.' She pressed a hand over the cynical

twist to his lips. All that she felt for him crowded to her own lips, but the woman had half awakened in her and she could no longer hero-worship Luque as she had done on the *Miranda*. She couldn't blurt out like a babbling child that she thought him the most marvellous man in the world, and that she didn't really care if he was as wicked as he made out. He accepted her as a person in her own right, and he didn't keep preaching. She would have loved him for that alone ... but there were other things about him that she loved. Secret things that her awakening heart whispered to her.

'I forbid you to have any illusions about me,' he said sternly. 'If you had not been so patently innocent aboard my yacht, I might well have taken advantage of you. But for once in my sinful life I held my predatory hand and let you act the boy for my amusement. As if any boy ever had such lashes,' he swept a finger along them, 'and this soft white skin, like something skimmed off the top of the milk.'

He sat there laughing at her, and because he meant to touch off her temper, she flared, 'Why didn't you tell me that you knew—laughing at me behind my back!' She slid down in her bed, grasping at the sheet to shield herself from his gibing eyes. 'Did you guess right away?'

'From the moment I carried you aboard the *Miranda*.'

'You knew I was a *girl*—was that why you took me aboard your boat?' Toni looked quite shocked and realised that he was capable of deeds that had only been whispered about at the convent, when Sister Imaculata was well out of earshot.

'Perhaps.' He shrugged his well-clad shoulders and stood up. 'I am now going to say *hasta luego, niña*. Don't let it worry you too much that I have a black

79

soul. I shall be as good to you as I am able, and you shall want for nothing, *golfo mio*. You shall know what it is to eat the delicious black roe of the sturgeon and the sparkling wine of the best vineyards, and I shall get a kick out of spoiling you. Yes, I shall spoil but not corrupt—if I can help it.'

With these ironical words he bent and slid a kiss over her red hair. 'I shall come for you Saturday morning and we'll drive to Mawgan Plas, where we shall shock all convention by being under the same roof before the nuptials. I can't be concerned with other people's ideas of what is right and what is wrong. It's a big house and you would be nervous there with just the servants, added to which it is already known that I had you with me on the *Miranda*.'

His odd eyes flickered a smile into her upraised eyes. 'You are already a scarlet woman, my little *ruad*. Do you mind terribly?'

She shook her head. All that mattered in the world was that he wanted her with him, in whatever capacity. Other people drifted like shadows on the edge of her consciousness ... Luque de Mayo ruled over her heart and soul.

She watched him stride from her room with his supple insouciance of body and mind. That he was capable of playing the devil she didn't doubt ... that he was also capable of a strange kind of tenderness she already knew.

When the door had closed behind his tall figure, leaving a curtain of blankness in the room, Toni sat up again and studied the ring he had placed on her left hand. It was absolutely gorgeous, but it also embarrassed her and she didn't want the nurse to see it. The woman would gossip about it to the other nurses and soon it would be all over the hospital that Luque de Mayo's funny little fiancée was weighted down with a diamond ring worth a considerable amount of money. Toni wanted to hide the ring, but where would it be safe from the inquisitive eyes of the blue and white dragon?

Toni glanced around the rather austere hospital room and noticed a cupboard over in a corner. She climbed out of bed, then gave a startled gasp as she felt the wobbly state of her legs and was glad when she reached the cupboard without falling over. She didn't fully realise that she was suffering from a combination of physical shock and nervous debility, brought on not only by the near-drowning but by the fact that she was not of the build that could stand persistently at a stone sink with her hands in water, or kneel scrubbing stone-floored corridors. She was coltish and fine-boned, and unaware that after the rescue from the water she had collapsed and lain in an exhausted sleep for thirty-six hours.

She clutched at the door handle of the cupboard and pulled it open. She stared at the cream leather vanity case that stood on a shelf, and fingered the folds of a fern-green dress with many fine pleats from the waist to the hem. There was also a coat of fine fawn cloth, and a suede cloche hat of a colour matching the dress. On the shelf beside the case stood a pair of suede shoes with delicate heels, matching the colour of the hat.

With shaking hands Toni opened the case and found inside a set of silk lingerie, a pair of cobweb-fine stockings, and a suspender-belt of white lace over elastic.

A complete outfit, beautiful and expensive and unlike anything Toni had ever seen in her deprived young life.

Feeling rather like Cinderella, she slid a bare foot into one of the shoes and found it a perfect fit.

Hers! Unbelievably hers from the crazy green hat to the wisp of a suspender-belt. She knew it instinctively, not only because the shoe fitted, but because of the colours and the way they expressed what she knew to be her own personality—a hint of the woods and the wild fawns running from their own shadows on swift, delicate hooves, half in fear of life, half in love with all the mystery and the hidden beauty.

Luque had provided these clothes for her, and tears stung her eyes at the way he looked after her. What did it matter if he didn't feel for her those strange, desperate desires that made life a hell or a heaven? He cared enough to want to keep her with him, and Toni was content, and she kissed her star-diamond before concealing it in a pocket of the fawn-coloured coat. It nestled deep in the silk lining, and with a sigh of relief she closed the cupboard door and made her wobbly way back to bed.

She was lazing there, feeling tired but happy, when her nurse came bustling into the room. She came to the bedside and regarded Toni with her usual look of curiosity and concern. 'All right, are you? Happy now you've seen his lordship and made certain he's alive and kicking?'

Toni nodded and her smile became reserved. It was her secret that she loved Luque with every tiny bit of her, and it was a relief that she had been able to hide his ring before the nurse's probing eyes got a glimpse of it. She was kind enough, but she obviously disapproved of Luque, and in Toni's eyes that was close to being a blasphemy. He was her lord, her deity ... the first person in her life to show her kindness without thrusting charity down her throat.

'He's taking me out of here on Saturday,' she said casually. 'It'll be nice to see something of Cornwall.'

'A stranger to the West Country, are you?' The nurse tidied the bedcovers which Toni had disturbed when she had got out of bed, pulling them taut over her slim figure. 'They say his lordship was sailing from Spain to visit Mawgan Plas, as he usually does about once a year, but there's nothing very Latin about you, not with that red hair.'

'I was living in Spain,' Toni said haughtily. 'That's where we met, if you must know.'

'What about parents—no one seems to mention any. A bit of a mystery, aren't you, my girl?'

Toni shrugged her shoulders, and already she had learned from Luque de Mayo that there was no need to explain herself to anyone. She belonged to him ... was answerable only to him. 'What's for tea?' she asked.

'Whatever you fancy, Miss Fleet.' The nurse gave a slight sniff, for she wasn't used to being snubbed by a bit of a girl who had somehow got her hooks into a rich man. 'You're here at *his* expense, so you can have a menu if you want one. I'll buzz the kitchen, shall I?'

'No,' Toni shook her head. 'You suggest something.'

'Well, how about sliced tomato sandwiches and a piece of apple-cake? You need fattening up, or you'll slip through the wedding ring when Lord Helburn puts it on your hand.'

'Lord—Helburn?' Toni felt as if she spoke the name aloud, but in truth she barely whispered it. It seemed so strange, and so impressive, and by marrying him she would become his lady.

The nurse gave Toni a frowning look, quite incapable of believing that the girl had no knowledge of his titled status. 'Yes, he came into the title when his English cousin broke his neck while sky-diving. Wild sort of family all round, and none too moral. His lordship's mother——'

'I know about his mother,' Toni broke in, a sudden blaze to her eyes. 'I know why she ran away from his father, so please don't scandalize her.'

'Sorry, I'm sure.' The nurse looked down into Toni's

eyes from which the haunting tints of green had vanished, leaving them sheer grey and stormy. 'Crazy about the man, aren't you? Well, if you'll take a bit of advice from a woman who's seen just about all there is to see of human nature, you'll take him down off his pedestal. Young girls will make idols of men, and it's a foolish and dangerous thing to do. Men aren't gods, duckie. More often than not they're devils, and that one of yours—heaven forbid that he's ever been nearer to a font than to have a drop of holy Roman water on his black head. I imagine you want the thrill of being a ladyship, but he won't be easy to live with.'

'No?' The storm-light faded from Toni's eyes and they became rather impudent. 'I'm willing to take the risk, and I bet you'd take it as well if he wanted you to marry him. Luque is attractive to women——'

'A bit too attractive, so you watch out.' The nurse spoke with a sort of triumph, having found a way to pull the magic carpet from under Toni's feet. 'You're no match for some of the women he's squired around, real society beauties with style to them and a classy way of wearing their clothes. I don't doubt that for a while you'll seem a novelty to him, but how long do novelties last? Until they break, my dear. Until they're pushed out of sight, and out of mind.'

With these words the nurse walked to the door. Instinct had informed her that Antonia Fleet was a girl from out of nowhere, and the human frailty of envy had made her cruel when she was usually kind.

'I'll see about your tomato sandwiches and a slice of cake,' she said, and the door closed behind her.

Toni shivered and no longer felt very hungry.

Novelties break ... novelties get pushed out of sight. The words spun around in her mind, and she suddenly curled down in her bed like a young animal seeking a hideaway, and pressed her hands over her ears.

But the words were inside her head and there was no shutting them out ... each word felt like a kick against her bowed young head. She couldn't argue against them, nor pretend that they hadn't the ring of a cruel and possible truth.

Luque hadn't pretended that their marriage was in any way a romantic one. She amused him and he felt responsible for her, but they weren't the emotions of love ... the kind of love that withstood all sorts of pressures that life could make upon a man and a woman.

Toni wanted with every particle of her lonely young heart to be with Luque, in whatever capacity he asked of her, but that didn't stop her from being terrified of what lay ahead of her. She was quite without a friend to whom she could turn for sympathy or advice, and right now she felt as she had long ago at the convent, one winter when she had caught cold and been ill all alone in the sick bay. Then, as now, an ice-cold awareness had gripped her that if she died there would be no one to break their heart over her.

You had to be loved for that to happen!

CHAPTER SIX

THE drive that led to the house had a will of its own, turning sharply, then twisting straight again, and all the time overshadowed by the great trees that must have been several centuries old. Their canopy closed out of the sun and strange shapes seemed to flit in and out of the path of the car, a powerful, sleek machine so in contrast with this air of an old world, where time had stood still.

So had this tree-shadowed drive led to Mawgan Plas in the days of the horse and carriage, and long before that, and Toni sat very quiet against the soft velour of her seat, but inwardly a hundred emotions were rushing through her veins. She longed to see the house in which Luque's mother had found some years of happiness with a man not her husband. She knew that the old scandal overhung the *plas*; she guessed that Cornish people would be in lots of ways like the Spanish, among whom she had grown up. Passionate and yet intolerant of those passions. Compassionate, and yet unforgiving of those who broke their rigid rules governing the control of the emotions. A strong, ruthless, handsome people, with long memories.

Only Luque would have the nerve to bring to this house yet another female who in their eyes was abandoned. It might pacify them that he meant to make a bride of her in the Church of the Lilies, but at this precise moment she was the latest 'flame' of wicked Lord Helburn. She was clad in the expensive silk garments he had bought, and on her left hand glowed his diamond ring.

'How did you know my size, Luque?' she asked. 'For the clothes—they fit as if made for me.'

'I had you measured, *chica*, while you lay in that long deathly sleep. In all my days I've never seen anyone sleep like that, as if in another world. I am sure the good nuns meant well, but they rather overworked you, little one. You aren't made for donkey work, not with your frame.'

'They were trying to improve me,' she said, with a touch of demureness. 'They considered that I had a wilful spirit, and Sister Imaculata felt that I should expiate my parents' sin.'

'That you stuck it so long as you did is a tribute to your staying power, but I still wonder at your angel of destiny for leading you across my path.' He flung her a side-glance and the tree shadows fell across his face, leaving only his eyes to gleam like odd gems in the dimness. 'If I had any sort of conscience I'd pass you on to some good-hearted soul and pay her to take care of you, but now it's too late for that. It looks as if I've ruined your reputation and had better make an honest woman of you.

'Woman?' He gave a sardonic laugh. 'You look in that hat and dress like a charming Peter Pan, and only the self-righteous would imagine you a victim of seduction. I admit to being one of the unscrupulous and I have played among the sirens and the cards stained with wine, but you have been in my keeping and there isn't a black mark on you, eh?'

'I'd like to tell everyone how good you've been to me,' she smiled, her hands clasped demurely in her lap though she longed to reach out and stroke away the lines of mockery beside his mouth.

'Then you'd ruin my reputation as a rake, and it's

taken me years to get such a satanic shine on it.'

'Oh, Luque,' she said, 'don't you ever want people to know that you can be—nice?'

'Nice?' he grimaced. 'Spare me that, *chica*. I'm about as nice as Barney's mischievous bull, and only an innocent like you would spot any gleams of gold in my intentions. It's well known that I suit only myself and that I do nothing that isn't in my own self-interest.'

'Like marrying me?' she asked, her stomach giving a curious twist as she said the incredible words. 'You mean you wouldn't do it just to stop people gossiping —you really want me—well, not *want* me——'

'Let's leave it there, Tonita, before you twist your tongue out of action. Let it suffice that you want to marry me, eh?'

'Yes,' she said faintly, knowing herself caught in the charisma of his personality and about as able to escape as a moth bound into the silken strands of a spider's web. She cared for him with too much heart to be able to make the struggle.

Snakes of ivy bound the great trees along the drive, and skull-cap flowers made ghostly rings at their bases. A small falcon-like bird flew from the branches crying: 'Bewitched ... bewitched ...' into the woods.

'Soon now you will see Mawgan Plas,' said Luque.

But first they came to the lodge at the gates, like an old enchanted cottage surrounded by elder trees and rhododendrons, sprawling in purple and blood-red masses, their bright pointing leaves a jungly mass. The slope of the roof, the time-weathered walls, the tiny panes of glass set in the windows, were so fascinating to Toni that she wished they might stop right here and not have to drive on to grander things.

A gaitered man at the gates saluted them, and Toni saw a long gun crooked against his arm and he wore a moleskin jacket as green and shiny as the lichen on the trees.

'That's Gwydh the gamekeeper,' said Luque. 'He and his wife live at the lodge—he had a small son who disappeared long ago, into the "beckoning golden sands" as the beach bogs are called. A morose fellow who does his work but rarely speaks to anyone. That's Cornwall for you, Toni, as it's Spain. Places of wild beauty and dark pain, where the belief rules that love is paid for, one way or another. Hide your love as you hide your sin, that is the rule, so remember it, *chica*.'

'Of course, *señor*,' she said, and her eyes were sad as she thought of the little boy running wild along the beach in search of shells and driftwood, one moment a carefree child with a live and beating heart, and the next a shadow on the sands as their wicked tremors closed over his day, his life.

A silence of sad enchantment had hold of her as the car sped from beneath the last pair of arching trees, in through a gothic gateway into a large rectangular courtyard of the *plas*.

It wasn't at all sombre, as Toni had rather expected, but picturesque with its angle-towers, balustraded roofs, and narrow doorways all white and black like a medieval chessboard. The sun lit the gothic points of the windows of a tower pointed and slender, with a cowled roof. A place out of a painting, not quite real, not even when Toni had climbed from the car and stood on the bottom step of the flight that led to the great front door with its wrought-iron knocker.

'Come!' Luque took her by the hand and led her up the steps, and when they reached the door she found that the knocker was in the form of a strange face with a diabolic stare that seemed to meet her own.

'Mawgan the wizard.' Even as Luque spoke he lifted the knocker and gave the door a resounding blow. 'They say he was a great rival of Merlin's, but that he made a magic that wrought mischief. The King at Tintagel was persuaded to order his destruction, and when the news reached Mawgan he disappeared and was only seen again as strange shapes in the woods of the *plas*. Superstitious little ass that you are, the story should appeal to you.'

'It does,' she said, biting her lip to be called a little ass just as a dignified manservant opened the door to them.

'Here we are, Lanyon. I hope you've provided an ample lunch, for the drive has given both of us a good appetite?'

'Indeed, sir. The cook said that you had given orders and I am sure she has carried them out to your satisfaction.' Lanyon spoke as he looked, with a precise dignity that didn't quite stop him from giving Toni a curious look. Expensively clad as she was, with the green hat pulled down at a perky angle, she still had an indefinable air of having come from an unworldly place where beautiful clothes, perfume and diamonds were never seen, let alone put on the body.

'This is Miss Fleet, Lanyon. She has been educated at a convent school and isn't quite at home in the outside world at present.'

'How do you do, miss?' The bishop-like figure gave Toni a brief bow.

In return she gave him a shy smile, and felt her hand gripped in Luque's a moment before she would have offered to shake hands with his butler. 'H-how do you do, Lanyon. Isn't Mawgan Plas a lovely big house? I thought it would be all stony and grey.'

'It is one of the more attractive houses of the region, miss,' he replied, in his very precise voice. 'A rare example of the Tudor in Cornwall, which makes it unusual to look at.'

'Lanyon is every inch an Englishman, Toni, but our

cook is so Cornish that she is called Tamsin, the Cinderella of the west country. She bakes the best meat and potato pasties I've ever tasted, a rare supper treat that makes any trip to Mawgan Plas worthwhile, even when a man has the misfortune to lose the *Miranda*.'

'A very sad misfortune, my lord.' Lanyon closed the front door, and Toni took a quick look around her and felt an immediate sense of history and mystery in the atmosphere of the beamed, black and white hall of the *plas*. House of a wizard ... of a woman who had flouted all the rigid marital rules of Spain ... and now of a man whose loveless boyhood had made him cynical, perhaps incapable of love himself.

'I hope, my lord, that the crew are now quite recovered?' Lanyon asked.

'All of them well and dried out, and as soon as the new yacht is rigged out they'll be back at work. At present they're taking a rest with relatives, all but my captain, who's seeing to it that the new sea lady is as sound and seaworthy as she looks. Yes, it's sad about the *Miranda*. I was fond of her, but there was no riding out a storm as furious as the one that sank her. We can only say *muchas gracias* to the fates for preserving our lives—this time.'

'Quite, sir. As it is almost lunchtime, shall I tell Cook to serve luncheon?'

'Yes, Lanyon, in the Chinese Room which is less overpowering than the dining-room, with all that Tudor oak and those curtains like purple coffin-drapes. I must have something done about that room—by the way, Tamsin has seen to it that Miss Fleet will be having the turret apartment overlooking the garden? The turret on the west side looks down on the sea and I don't want her to be reminded too much of our encounter with the Cornish waves.'

At this request Lanyon suddenly looked disconcerted, and Toni felt the glance that he shot at her, perhaps hinting that she wasn't quite the nervous innocent that Luque made her out to be.

'The trouble is, my lord, that we have had trouble with the roof of the garden turret, some of the old tiles having slipped in that severe storm, letting in the rain. There are damp patches, sir, and it isn't in good condition at present.'

'Then why the devil didn't you send for a repair man?' Luque demanded.

'I did, my lord, immediately Tamsin said you had requested that the garden turret be made ready for the young lady. I couldn't get in touch with you, sir, as you had gone to London and not left the address at which you would be staying, and so I couldn't inform you that the roofing man had to order tiles to match the existing ones, and it will be several more days before they can be delivered.'

'Well, there are other rooms in the house, Lanyon.' There was a click as Luque lit a cheroot, and Toni felt sure he had tensed, sharply, when his butler had mentioned his trip to London. She didn't want to care too much that he hadn't mentioned it to her ... why should he, when she had no place in the life that he led away from her?

'The fact is, my lord, that Tamsin prepared the sea turret instead, and has made it look so pleasant——'

There, before Luque could speak, Toni broke in on Lanyon who was obviously trying to spare Tamsin any more work on behalf of the fiancée whom Luque had sprung upon them. She didn't want the staff to think her a finicky, highly-strung creature who was going to be more of a nuisance than a mistress. She wanted to love Mawgan Plas, and she wanted to be liked, just a little.

'I shan't mind sleeping in sound of the sea, Lanyon.'

She caught at Luque's arm and gave him a smile from eyes that reflected the colour of her green hat. 'I'm not at all nervous, *señor*. I shan't have any nightmares.'

'You had better not,' he said grimly. 'All right, Lanyon, you can assure Tamsin that Miss Fleet will sleep in the apartment prepared for her, and now we'll have our food. This afternoon there should be a delivery of several packages from London, so you will take the estate car and fetch them from the station.'

'Very well, sir.' The butler went away with his stately stride, and Toni allowed her smile to travel to her lips, flicking off her hat as she accompanied Luque to a door at the opposite side of the hall, beside which stood a curious figurine on a low black table.

'Kuan Yin, the goddess of mercy.' Luque gestured at the Chinese figure with slightly bowed head and clasped hands. 'You may have need of her.'

'Why, because I can't expect any from you?' Toni threw him a look as she walked past him into the room. 'I promise you, *señor*, that I shall never trouble you with my naïve fears. I know they would only be a bother and a bore for a man of the world.'

'And that remark really shows your naïveté,' he drawled, as he came into the Chinese Room behind her and closed the door. 'The female of the species always assumes that she has certain secrets that no male can ever understand. It's a fallacy, my darling. We men do know how we came into the world, and that by reason of her biology a woman is as strange as the moon, as the sea, and the tides. Why do you say I'd be bored by your fears?'

'Because you said I'd better have no nightmares.' Toni looked around her and found herself in a room so unusual, so beautiful, that she caught her breath. She stood there entranced, for the austerity of convent life had not prepared her for wall panels of hand-painted silk, on which paradise-birds shone and quivered. Nor had she ever seen cupboards of tulipwood and lacquer, inset with tiny clusters of drawers, delicately painted with pavilions and figures in shades of gold and softly glowing brown. Between long windows that led into a walled garden there was a low lacquered table on which stood a lovely bowl adorned with persimmon and birds, rockwork and foliage; tiny gilt shell-feet holding the bowl.

'My mother's lover was a man of artistic temperament, remember.' Lean hands closed over Toni's shoulders and she quivered like one of those paradise-birds, and she stood very still as the lean fingers unbuttoned her coat and drew it off her slim figure. He laid the coat over the carved back of a sofa whose cushions were covered with the hand-painted Chinese silk, and with a sort of shyness, because this was the first time she had stood before him in a dress, Toni ruffled her hair with her fingers and felt acutely aware of herself as Luque ran his eyes over her.

'Nicer to be in silk, eh, than the chopped-down trousers of my steward? You look rather like a young Irish page, though I don't imagine that the good Sister who cut your hair under a pudding-basin had that impression in mind. H'm, well-turned ankles, slim straight legs, a boy's hips, but a girl's neck, pale and shadowed against the green silk. You will suffice as my Lady Helburn, and to hell with those who will say that I'm a hundred years too old for you.'

'Don't exaggerate,' she tried to smile, but her lips quivered with nerves. 'People are going to say that you must be mad to marry a nobody, which is what I am, *señor*.'

'*Niña mia*, if a lord can't do as he damn well likes, then who the devil can? For me it would be hell on

94

earth to marry a lady, so-called, armed to the elbows with diplomas of birth, breeding and bed. I'd probably have one hell of a week with her, and then spend the rest of our lives being impolitely bored by her hunting and shooting friends.'

'That isn't the complete picture, *señor*.' Toni walked to the windows that looked upon the charming rock-garden set within a circle of walls on which hung yards of ivy polished by the sun. 'There has to be someone whom you love——'

'Myself,' he said curtly. And the next moment in his silent way he came to the window behind her, and his cheroot smoke drifted across the top of her head. 'Don't become a probing, inquisitive woman just yet, *golfo*. I prefer you as you are.'

His left hand slid down and gripped her waist. Her left hand reached out uncertainly and gripped a fold of the silk curtains, and at once the rays of sunlight found the diamonds of her ring and set them shimmering.

'You haven't said whether you like your ring. I hope you do, for I went all the way to London to buy it.'

'It's beautiful, but you didn't have to—I mean, I didn't expect a ring, least of all a diamond one.'

'What did you expect?' There was an edge to his voice. 'Paste and brass, my pet, on the hand that I hold in mine? Knowing my arrogance you should know better than that. I have an acute distaste for cheap imitations, so you can take it from me that the diamond star and its satellites are perfectly real, and from a jewellers in Mayfair. No brass for my bride, nor any of the jewels that lie locked away in Spain. Let them rot, those rubies like blood, those emeralds green as fear!'

He moved away from her as he spoke, taking savage

paces across the oriental carpet. 'The long shadows of old sins, Toni. They stretch, they reach out and cast a darkness on the spirit. Don't love me ... and don't seek to be loved by me, do you hear? Be the bride of my English side, and don't ever meddle with my Spanish passions, for they aren't to be trusted!'

As his words died away into a rather shocking silence, there came a polite knock on the door and it opened to admit Lanyon. He carried a folded table and he was followed by a gawky boy carrying a pair of chairs.

'I wondered, my lord, if you would like your luncheon served outside in the sunshine?'

Luque was in control of himself in a moment and that dark look was instantly gone from his face. 'By all means,' he said. 'It's always a pity to waste the sunlight when it chooses to shine for us.'

Lanyon and the boy went out into the walled garden, and Toni watched from half-lowered lashes as Luque extinguished his cheroot in an ashtray, grinding it slowly and mercilessly into brown pieces. She was caught between flight towards him, and flight away from him ... in this mood he was like a tiger with a thorn in him, and there was no getting near him to help him. She was too uncertain, too untried, and so she played safe and stepped through the open windows into the garden, and watched as the table was set beneath a tree, the sunlight falling in daggers of gold through the hot still leaves.

While she watched the ritual, a scent of clambering roses trapped in the warm air, a lace cloth was brought, and things of silver that glittered in the stabs of sunlight. Toni was fascinated, comparing the lovely Chinese plates and the silver cutlery with the thick earthenware and the dull metal of the long convent tables in the whitewashed refectory, the conversation of the girls muted by the presence of a Sister at each end of the table, making sure that the slabs of brown bread were shared out fairly and that each bowl of vegetable soup was consumed to the last drop.

Toni's first lunch at Mawgan Plas was memorable for several reasons, but when Luque joined her at the table the moody look had lifted from his face, and he quirked an appreciative eyebrow as he tasted the wine that Lanyon served with their trout in parsley butter, hot and steaming on a silver dish in the shape of a fish.

'Excellent,' said Luque, and his glance was upon Toni as the pale gold wine was poured into the stemmed glass that stood beside her plate. On board the *Miranda* she had not dined with him, and so it felt strange, and curiously intimate, to find herself seated at table with him. She tried not to show her feelings in her eyes as she looked at him, so casually at ease in his single-breasted suit with a pin-striped silk shirt and bow tie. At his wrists were cuff-links with square dark stones, and his fingernails were cut close and square. He wore no rings, yet that pride of race, so essentially Spanish, was stamped on his face. It was there in the lean strength of his features; a suggestion of arrogance and great passion about the lips; a strain of severity and obstinacy in the set of the jaw. It was his eyes that revealed the bewildering aspects of his character; in them lay his mixed blood, his divergent emotions; his danger and his charisma.

'We must drink a toast to our future, Toni,' he said, as the discreet Lanyon left them alone. 'Shall it be in English or Spanish?'

'I leave it to you, Luque,' she said, her fingers tight and nervous about the stem of her wine glass.

'Then let it be in English, and let it be this, Tonita. "Life is a jest and all things show it. I thought so once,

97

but now I know it." A poet called Gay wrote that, and anyone who accepts it is infinitely consoled.'

'Then I'll accept it, *señor,* if you wish me to do so.'

'I wish it, Tonita.' And very solemnly they clinked glasses, an amused glint to his eyes as he watched the cautious way Toni sipped her wine.

'It's delicious,' she murmured, and felt a pang of guilt at the way she was taking to worldly pleasures. She put down the glass as if to deny the delicious warmth of the wine, and the sharp sort of sweetness. Luque gave his brief, sardonic laugh, as if he knew what motivated her.

'Come,' he mocked, 'you're not wishing for water and mutton stew, are you, after taking a chance on breaking your neck? Convent walls are high because virtue has a very human way of being rebellious. Little one, there's no need to feel guilty about a dish of trout and a glass of wine ... unless you'd like me to return you to your life of self-denial?'

'No ...' She looked horror-stricken. 'I couldn't bear it!'

'What, the self-denial?' His eyebrow was quirked as he carried a fork to his lips, a piece of trout speared on the silver prongs.

'No ... being a nun!' Her throat went so dry that she caught at her glass and gulped her wine. 'I—I'm very wicked ... it's in my blood, I suppose.'

At this he really laughed, but there was no underlying amusement in his laughter. 'My absurd child, you have no conception of wickedness, so eat your fish before it gets cold and the butter goes brittle.'

She obeyed him, and in a while she felt a little less tense and was glad that he talked not about themselves but about the Cornish environs of Mawgan Plas, the rolling moorlands with their granite tors and lost-in-time villages, where great cliffs reared above a sea that ranged from deep blue to sheerest emerald. On the moors stood the menhirs that were said to be petrified witches and warlocks, to whom the superstitious still made offerings, and those who walked alone there, through the heather and the gorse, whistled as they went and never looked behind them.

'Do you often walk alone there?' Toni asked him, glancing up from the steak and vegetable pie that had followed the trout. She hadn't known until meeting Luque that lunch could consist of more than one dish of food, so perfectly cooked that each mouthful was a pleasure. And not only that, the dishes were taken away when empty and there was no awful prospect of a great mound of plates and bowls to be washed in a deep stone sink, standing in her flat shoes on a hard stone floor. Often ... a little too often she had gone to bed with aching feet and ankles, and in the winter time there had been chilblains on her hands.

Oh, Luque, she thought, if it's wicked being here with you and it makes a lost soul of me, then I shall just have to bear the hellfire when it comes!

'Yes, I've walked alone on the moors,' he said, with his cryptic smile. 'And if you're wondering if I've ever looked back, then the answer is no. I never look back, Tonita, for I might look myself in the face.'

'You speak in riddles, *señor*.'

'Which is just as well, for young girls shouldn't learn all the answers all at once. They are more amusing when they're a little dumb, and a little wise, and it's only the older type of woman who fascinates by the wisdom which life has taught her.'

'You sound as if you dislike intellectuals, *señor*, if they are women.'

'Most men do,' he drawled. 'The cleverest women hide it and create an aura of wit and charm instead. Those who can't wait a moment to prove how much smarter than men they are—*Dios*, what bores! A man might as well invite a bearded professor to lunch than a female with all her mental pencils sharpened; instead of being an amusing companion she sits for an examination, gobbling food and words and waving her hands about like a merchant in a bazaar. It is probably the Spaniard in me that dislikes the type!'

Toni couldn't help smiling at the look on his face. 'Do Englishmen like intellectual women?' she asked.

'Not if they have any sense, but they have such a high measure of tolerance that it's likely they endure such women out of sheer gallantry. It would be like kissing a Roget's Thesaurus!'

'And you prefer to kiss a woman who is dumb?' Toni said demurely.

He gave her a quick look at that and his eyes narrowed, gem-points that almost felt as if they pricked her skin. 'Have you ever been kissed, Tonita?' he asked suddenly.

She let her mind rove back and forth down the years, and it gave her an odd feeling to realise that not once in her life had anyone put their arms about her and kissed her with love. Luque had briefly kissed her cheek when he had given her the diamond ring, but such a caress didn't really count. He didn't love her ... not in the truest sense of the word. He merely wished to have a wife who would leave him free to lead his own life.

She shook her head. 'Kisses are not encouraged in convents,' she said. 'Not for foundlings, who have to learn to accept charity and duty as their daily bread.'

'My poor child, we had better remedy such a deprivation.' And even as he spoke he pushed back his chair and came round to her side of the table, and as she looked up startled he bent his tall head and placed a kiss on her partly open lips. His lips were warm and firm, and just a little peppery, and there shot through Toni such a rare sensation that her lips stayed in their kissed position, as if inviting him to do it again.

'More,' he drawled softly, 'like Oliver Twist and the porridge?'

'It's an odd business,' she murmured. 'One connects the mouth with eating—somehow.'

'My innocent one, kissing is a kind of hunger.' But this time his mouth touched hers in the very lightest caress, as if she were the dessert in his life, never the main meal. And in defiance of this she wanted to throw her arms about his neck and hold him to her. She didn't ask to be loved, not if he found that kind of love too bitter to his taste. But she didn't want to be treated—always—as a lost puppy whom it pleased him to lead about in a diamond collar.

'Child,' his hands gripped hers and he drew away with a curt laugh, 'don't develop a taste for that kind of thing; it can lead to dyspepsia of the soul and ennui of the spirit.'

'For you,' she rejoined. 'You've kissed all kinds of women and you're jaded, but I've spent my days being chastened. It felt—nice when you kissed me.'

'Did it?' For a brief moment something flamed in his eyes, to be immediately extinguished by his lashes. 'You're getting out of hand, my puppy, since I've been feeding you on meat, I kissed you as I'd stroke a pup, so you remember it and don't start rolling on your back with your begging paws in the air—it can be dangerous.'

He strode back to his chair and pushing aside his plate he sat toying with his wine glass. Toni cast him a quick look and saw that his gaze dwelt broodingly upon a great clump of blue scabious against a wall ... the plant that if picked brought the devil to your bedside!

Footsteps approached across the paving of the walled garden, breaking into the silence that was discordant rather than harmonious, and when Toni glanced in the direction of the footfalls she was startled to see a formidable-looking woman thrusting past Lanyon, who hovered uncertainly near the windows of the Chinese Room. The woman was followed by a fair girl in cream chiffon printed with blue flowers.

'Oh . . .' said Toni.

Luque turned his head and scowled. 'Hell!' he muttered, and there was a definite savagery in the way he rose to his feet as the woman sailed towards him. 'Aunt Charlotte, what an unexpected—pleasure!'

'Is it really?' She gave him a haughty look. 'I had to learn from the newspapers that you were in England —that you were nearly drowned in the process of bringing your fiancée home. Is that the girl?'

'The one and only,' he drawled. 'The wedding takes place next Friday—have you any objections, my dear aunt?'

'A number of them!' The woman stared at Toni, probing her face with hard and arrogant eyes, sweeping them over her hair, and up and down her body.

The girl in chiffon was also giving Toni a thorough examination. 'She's a new type for you, isn't she, Luque? And where on earth does she get her hair done? Does she go to the barber who sees to the choirboys?'

'You're out of your mind, Luque!' His aunt spoke so cuttingly that Toni flinched. 'It's one thing to have this—this girl on the *Miranda* with you, but you can't possibly make her your wife.'

'You don't say?' He spoke without raising his voice, but there was an edge to it, like thin and cutting steel. 'I wonder who is going to stop me?'

'Anyone can see that she's totally unsuitable, and

you know it, Luque. A little Miss Mystery whom nobody seems to know a thing about—with red hair, of all things!'

'Quite appropriate if she's going to be Lady Helburn.' His hands were steady as steel as he extracted a cheroot from his case and held his lighter to it. 'Hell and flames are red, aren't they?'

'I didn't come here to listen to your peculiar brand of cynicism,' his aunt snapped. 'A man in your position can't marry a *nobody*!'

Toni clenched the edge of the table and felt like a duck being vivisected alive and quivering. She hadn't known that relatives could be so unpleasant ... it was shattering to discover that family relationships weren't always warm and tolerant, and she who had no one could almost feel glad, if this were the reality.

'What an enormous sparkler!' The girl in flowered chiffon was staring at Toni's left hand. 'Have you been parting with the family heirlooms already, Luque?'

It was this remark which brought Toni to her feet. 'Luque,' she spoke with a touch of desperation, 'I'd better leave you to a family conference and vanish for a while. Perhaps Lanyon can show me my room?'

'No, you stay here with me.' He reached for her hand and pulled her to his side, and as Toni felt the hard locking of his fingers around hers, she gave in to him and heard his aunt draw in her breath with almost a hissing sound.

'The wedding will not be a white one, Aunt,' he said, 'nor will there be one of those awful receptions that drag on through a lot of inept jokes and speeches. Toni and I are flying off to Paris as soon as the ceremony is performed, therefore it would be a waste of time to ask any of the family to attend.'

'I—see.' His aunt was staring at Toni, mentally stripping the fern-green dress from her slim shape.

'Why the hurry, Luque? Is the girl in trouble? She appears to be a naïve creature, but there's something in her eyes that isn't so innocent. I never did care for green eyes——'

'I need hardly point out, Aunt, that you don't have to care for them. As it happens Toni's eyes are grey-green and very Irish, and she is also that rare creature in our society, a mental and physical virgin!'

A seething silence followed Luque's words, punctuated by drifts of cheroot smoke. 'Of course, it's your idea of a twisted joke,' his aunt snapped. 'Has she the social graces, the innate poise of a lady? No! And where does she come from—dare you tell us that?'

'It's really none of your business,' he drawled. 'And as for the social graces, they're just a concealment for every kind of social vice. It's probably quite true to say that Toni hasn't a shade of vice in her, and for all I care she can spill her coffee on the carpet, wear jeans to Ascot, and a string of pearls in the bath. She's Eliza to my Professor Higgins, and nothing you can say or do will alter the fact that come next Friday she will become the next Lady Helburn.'

CHAPTER SEVEN

AGAIN there was a silence that seemed to stretch the nerves to a painful tension, while somewhere in a flower a bee buzzed angrily.

'I see that you've made up your mind!' Luque's aunt was breathing hard, so that her bosom strained against her silk coat. 'You must be under the spell of the girl —a man of your age!'

'Toni, go off with Birdina for a while.' He spoke lazily and uncurled his fingers from hers. 'Have a look around the *plas*, but if Birdy tries to insult you, then scratch her back. She wouldn't be a bad sort of girl, if she'd ever washed a few thousand greasy plates and washed a few floors.'

Toni glanced enquiringly at Birdina, who was giving Luque an inquisitive look. 'Is that how your fiancée learned her virtue,' she asked him pertly, 'washing up and scrubbing?'

'Make no mistake, Birdy, she has virtue, but she also has a temper, so mind your manners.' And with a dismissive wave of his hand at the two girls, he turned his attention to his aunt. With a sense of reluctance Toni fell into step beside Birdina and made no attempt to start a conversation as they made their way down some twisting stone steps that led from the walled garden to a lower section of the grounds.

A multitude of rock plants overhung the sloping sides of the steps and freckled bees flew in and out of the flower heads. They didn't worry Toni, who had often worked with the bee-keeper at the convent, but Birdina kept shying nervously away from the honey-gatherers.

'I'm not what you'd call the country type,' she said. 'I told my mother it would be a wasted journey to come and argue with Luque, but when she gets a bee in her bonnet there's no shifting her from her purpose —I suppose it runs in the family. She had you tagged as some common little gold-digger—you know what the newspapers are and how they can make black seem like dirty grey. You don't look common.'

'Thanks,' said Toni. 'Now do I stand on my hind-legs and wag my tail?'

Birdina gave a side-glance at Toni as they paused on a half-moon terrace above the sea. There was a cove down below and spray was being flung high over a ridge of jagged rocks, embedded in the sand at the edge of the beach. 'Is Luque in love with you?' she asked.

Love! Toni's heart gave an uncomfortable throb, for the question was unexpected. Her hands closed over the rough stonework of the terrace and the sun winked in her ring, almost mockingly.

'I mean,' Birdina faced her, fixing inquisitive eyes upon her face, 'just between us, have you slept with him, and is he as fabulous as he looks? He's a very sexy-looking man, is my half-Spanish cousin.'

'What do you mean—sexy? I think he has personal magnetism.' Toni looked away from Birdina and stared at the sea. 'He told your mother the truth—he hasn't laid a hand on me.'

'Luque? Why, he has a terrible reputation with regard to women. One of them got him mixed up in her divorce and there was a fearful scandal because she was married to a Spanish diplomat. I believe they had a fight, for this Spaniard was seen around with his arm in a sling and it was whispered that Luque had broken his arm. There isn't much he isn't capable of, but you aren't going to tell me he took you on the *Miranda* just to give you a holiday!'

'That's exactly what he did.' Toni looked at Birdina with eyes as clear as the sea, with little hints of jade in them. 'I don't think anyone really knows Luque—perhaps he doesn't fully know himself—but he's been wonderfully good to me.'

'Well, strangely enough I believe you.' Birdina looked amazed. 'Has the rake reformed, or is he saving you up for a feast after the famine?'

'I—I don't like this kind of talk.' Toni flushed. 'Doesn't anyone believe in love any more? Has it become just a cheap pleasure?'

'My dear, you talk like someone out of a nunnery. Is that it? Has Luque reverted to full Spanish instincts and got himself a bride out of a convent? I do believe that's what the devil would do! They say, don't they, that the devil only loves innocence so he can destroy it?'

'Th-that isn't true!' Toni went so white that her eyes blazed a sheer green. 'That isn't the reason Luque is marrying me!'

'Why else would he?' Birdina gave a trill of laughter. 'He's tried every other form of amusement, so why not revert to true character and do as his father did? You're the little shorn lamb he's leading to perdition, dear!'

Toni felt a rip of anguish, like a claw tearing her heart. The cruel flippancy of the words went right through her ... all the more edged because Luque himself never denied the devil in him.

'I say, you have gone white!' Birdina touched the glittering ring on Toni's hand. 'When the wolf comes slinking by, the sensible little lamb makes a bolt back to the fold where she came from. You're not cut out for the smart life, comic-cute as you look in your green silk dress, with your hair cut straight across your brow like some choirboy in an old print. One can see that a man might find you—intriguing, but when it comes to being a lady of society—my dear, you'll be a disaster. It will be hell for you, having to hold your own with the kind of people Luque is obliged to mix with. You'd have to entertain; be the hostess at dinner parties and garden soirées. I can't see you doing it, for there's more to being Luque's lady than sailing about the high seas with him.'

'Is there?' Toni looked straight at Birdina, her chin tilted as she strove not to be cowed down by this barrage of raw truths. 'I suppose you fancy yourself in the role, having been trained to insult people with a smile on your face—people whom you imagine to be inferior to you? What a pity Luque doesn't fancy you!'

At this retaliation Birdina's lips thinned into a pair of pink-painted lines, and her eyes sharpened so they looked an enamelled blue. 'He said his little scrubbing girl had a temper, didn't he? Have you ever seen him lose his? Luque might have the polish of an English gentleman, but he's a Spaniard at heart, and there's cruel blood in his veins. Men like him aren't easy to live with, and he could be hell let loose when the joke wears thin and he finds himself tied to a sexless little chit with the body of a boy!'

Birdina stood away and looked Toni up and down, and she gave a scornful laugh. 'Yes, it's plain as a pikestaff what Luque is up to. He never forgave the Helburns for ignoring his mother, especially when she fell ill and no one let him know. He's wanted to get his own back for a long time, and so he's going to marry you—a naïve nobody with not a drop of *sangre azul* in your veins, not a penny in the bank, and hardly built to produce a baby Helburn—unless you die in the attempt.'

Toni shuddered ... it was as if Birdina threw darts at her and they pierced her skin, letting in poison that ran bitter and deadly through her veins.

'You say that the Spanish side of Luque is cruel,' she said. 'What of the Helburn side? It seems abominably cruel to me that his mother's family kept it from him that she was ill—that she was going to die. I can understand his bitterness——'

'Are you going to be so understanding when he takes a mistress?' Birdina smiled thinly and took a gold powder-case from her handbag; she studied her face in the little mirror and patted the smooth fair waves that framed her pert features. 'He will, you know. He's a man of experience and he's accustomed to women of wit, beauty and sensuality. I wonder how you'll cope with that situation when it arises? Any ideas?'

'I—I just don't believe that Luque is as predatory, unprincipled and reckless as you make out.' Toni spoke with a touch of dignity that concealed a riot of doubts and fears. The life ahead of her seemed as beset with hidden dangers as the sea that shimmered below Mawgan Plas, holding silver and shadow in equal measure; holding magic and madness.

'Then you must be in love with him.' Birdina shrugged her shoulders and her blue-flowered chiffon blew in a soft gust of sea wind; a fragile material covering a personality that was also volatile. Love for Birdina would never be self-sacrifice ... as it had to be for Toni.

'It must be a new and amusing experience for Luque, to find himself on a pedestal, looked up to as some kind of a god. What did he do to earn all the adulation—save you from a fate worse than death?' Birdina gave a giggle that wasn't really girlish, for it held a little too much scratch and not enough purr.

Fate ... yes, fate had been there at that Spanish fair, lurking in a mask at the saturnalia, stalking her in a spiked heel.

'He saved my life,' Toni said quietly.

'How fearfully romantic,' drawled Birdina, closing her powder-case with a sharp little snap. 'So now you belong to him, body and soul. His adoring acolyte, who even looks the part. What are you going to wear for the wedding?'

'I—I don't yet know,' Toni admitted. 'I expect Luque will arrange about my dress——'

'You must be kidding?' Birdina looked at Toni as if she couldn't believe her ears. 'Does he take charge of everything—I say, I wouldn't care for that. It's the man's place to pay, but the girl's pleasure to choose the goodies that he pays for. You've a lot to learn, Toni, and permitting a man to be your master is asking for trouble. I'll admit that Luque has impeccable taste when it comes to clothes, and I suppose he chose that dress you have on, but a wedding dress is a different matter—my dear, don't you know that it's unlucky for the groom to even see the dress before the two of you meet at the altar?'

Toni gave a little shiver ... she was beginning to think that it would take a miracle for her marriage to be blessed with good luck.

'You know, you're inclined to infuriate me.' For the first time the sharp look was gone from Birdina's eyes and she was regarding Toni with a certain sympathy. 'If you were Goody-Two-Shoes I'd hate you, but there's something about you, it's there in your eyes— something elusive, original, I don't know! If you're a gold-digger, then you're a new one on me!'

'Thanks, but I don't want any roses from you,' Toni said, 'not after the rocks you've been throwing.'

'Why, do you bruise so easily?' Birdina asked pertly.

'Did he get you out of a convent, straight out of the wrappings of a pure upbringing? Yes, your eyes give you away! I bet he's the first man you've ever had any dealings with, and the Latin in Luque would revel in that. Was it one of those strict places in Ireland—he said you were Irish, didn't he?'

'Yes, but I was a—a pupil at a Spanish convent,' Toni said, and wondered what sort of a look would have come over Birdina's face if she told her the real truth. 'I was put there when I was quite young—when I lost my parents.'

'You don't say?' Birdina looked intrigued. 'I've never known a girl from a convent, least of all one who has recently left after being there for years. Why, that makes you a veritable *nun!*'

'Not quite.' Toni had to smile. 'I never had that kind of saintliness.'

'No, but you're terribly innocent. Did they tell you about life—about men and women, and how babies come to be born?'

'Yes, we were told.' Toni recalled those lessons, the facts that were outlined in bare and biological language. There had been no discussion of the love inherent in the ideal relationship; the nuns had known too well that most of their pupils were going out into the world as the brides of men chosen for them by their parents: men they hardly knew and would have to learn to know *after* the wedding.

'Was it embarrassing, to be told those kind of things by women who had taken vows of chastity?' Birdina was all agog, and much more likeable now she had dropped her air of being a woman of the world. 'I really don't know how anyone can go through life without some romance and love in it. It must be terribly sterile, never to put your arms around a man and have him kiss the breath out of you. I couldn't stand it. I mean, a woman is flesh and blood, not a stone angel, and I love those shivery thrills that one gets when a man just looks, let alone touches!'

'I might have become a nun,' Toni said quietly. 'I was meant for the life of chastity and charity—oh, it all seems to have happened in another life and I don't really care why Luque is marrying me. I seem to belong to him, and that's all I know.'

Birdina stared at Toni, whose face in that moment had the strange terror and beauty of someone walking into flames.

'I say, it's all a bit too deep for me.' Birdina forced a laugh, and then glanced across the terrace to where the stone steps led down from the house. A tall figure in smooth grey suiting appeared, and when he caught sight of the two girls he broke into a baffling smile, his harlequin eyes shifting from one slim figure to the other, where they rested on the sunlit red hair ... hair that shone like a flame against the white neck and the high-shadowed cheekbones.

'Lanyon is about to drive to the station, so he'll be taking you and your mother, Birdy.' His gaze flickered back to his young cousin. 'I did intimate that you would be welcome to the wedding, but she fears for your innocence, so you had better go home with her.'

'Mother is a bore!' Birdina flew to him and clutched his arm. 'I'd love to stay, Luque! I've never been to the wedding of someone who nearly became a nun! It's strange, exciting, and something I can't miss!'

'I'm afraid your mama is adamant that you go home with her, and it really won't be much of a wedding, Birdy. A few brief words at the altar, a ring on the hand, and then we'll be away for our—honeymoon.'

Birdina pouted up at him, her pink lips pleading with him—and, so it seemed to Toni, inviting him. His swarthy face was bent to the girl's fair one, and

Toni was stabbed by the realisation that many curvaceous lips had known the feel of Luque's hard mouth. His lean strong arms had held slender bodies in surrender to him, their senses and their souls in thrall to his strange charm. Like Harlequin he had gone his careless way through the ranks of the foolish Columbines . . . and for his bride he chose Pierrette, the half-sad clown who lurked in the shadows of joy.

'Oh, Luque, you always manage to get your own way! I want to stay with you and Toni!'

'Why, curious?' He quirked an eyebrow and shot a quick look at Toni. 'Has my *novia* been letting a few cats out of the bag?'

'I wheedled a whisker or two out of Toni,' Birdina admitted, giving him a coy smile. 'Fancy you playing Don Quixote and rescuing a maiden from fearful chastity!'

'A rare good deed in a bad life, Birdy, but chastity is such a rare gem that I couldn't let it out of my hands once I had it. I really began to think that it didn't exist, but I'm afraid your mother and I have had such a slanging match that you won't be allowed to stay under my roof.'

'You mean you've had a fight over Toni?'

'Quite. She has washed her hands off the pair of us and consigned us to the devil himself. She awaits you, chicken, so you had better fly off with her, back to your smart little coop in Belgravia.'

'Luque, sometimes you have a way of saying things that makes me want to cry——'

'Heaven forbid, Birdy! Your mascara will run all down your cheeks and spoil a very pretty picture. Let it be enough that your mother and I have had one of our annual disagreements and I don't want to upset her further by going against her wishes with regard to you. One day, *niña*, you will have a large and glamorous wedding of your own, but Toni and I are tying the knot as quickly and quietly as possible. We'll even wait to have our champagne in Paris.'

'Is that how Toni wants it?' Birdina spoke a little sulkily. 'She doesn't even know what she's wearing for the wedding.'

'She will know.' He said it almost carelessly, as if Toni played a very minor role in the drama of their marriage. 'Unlike you, Birdy, my *novia* is quite happy in a pair of jeans and a shirt and sets no great store by the vanities of our materialistic world. Therein lies her peculiar charm. I shan't be constantly plagued by a wife whose happiness lies in the accumulation of enough silks, sables and scents to stock out a pasha's harem.'

'Then I only hope,' said Birdina, with a toss of her carefully waved hair, 'that the man I marry doesn't regard me as a form of economy. Poor Toni, I envied her for a while, but she's welcome to you, Luque, if you're going to treat her so meanly. I'd want to be something special to my husband—I'd want him to spoil me, with—with fearful abandon.'

'What man could do otherwise?' He smiled enigmatically. 'Never fear, Birdy, you'll find someone to keep you cooing with lots of baubles and beads.'

'I should hope so!' Yet Birdina gave Luque a rather calculating look, as if she found something a little suspect in his words. The look he returned her was perfectly bland and suave, a glimmer of mockery in his odd eyes. 'No wonder Mother finds you such an infuriating man, Luque. You go your own way completely, don't you?'

'If I can possibly manage it, *niña*.'

'Marching to the devil's drumbeat, Mother says!'

'Mother would. And now say a nice goodbye to Toni before your mother comes thundering down those steps after you.'

'You're a terrible man,' Birdina flung at him. 'I hope, at least, that you'll allow your shorn lamb a few francs so she can send me a postcard from Paris!'

'My shorn lamb?' His eyebrow rose in a quizzing peak above an eye as black as onyx, and very deliberately he turned his head and studied the girl who leaned against the rough stonework of the terrace wall, the sky blending with the sea at the back of her slim shoulders. 'I will admit that she's a trifle shorn, Birdy, but she's no lamb. She's more of a winged thing—a dragonfly, perhaps, which emerges from its shell with iridescent wings too easily damaged by the winds of chance. Life isn't easy for dragonflies, but they offer their moments of startling strangeness.'

Birdina listened to him with a completely blank expression, as if he had broken into a language alien to her. 'Oh, what nonsense you do talk, Luque!'

'And how like Aunt Charlotte you can sound, my pet. Beware!'

'Rats,' she said inelegantly. 'I sometimes think Mother's right when she says there's a crazy streak in the Helburns and you have it. Well, I'm off in case it's catching. Goodbye, Toni! I hope you like Paris ...' With a swirling of chiffon skirt Birdina was gone, running lightly away into the sunlight, a bright bird of a girl whose feelings and thoughts were not of the deep kind. ''Bye ... have fun!' Floating back to them like the airy calling of a bird.

'And that was Birdina,' Luque drawled as he strolled towards Toni. 'Decorative enough, but she's never been encouraged to spread her mental wings. Her mother, of course, is a thundering snob, and I hope you didn't take her remarks too much to heart.'

'She came as a bit of a shock,' Toni admitted. 'It didn't occur to me that any of your relatives would suddenly descend on us.'

'Like the locusts on the corn, eh? That woman will sell her own daughter into the bondage of a material marriage, but my mother must be eternally damned because she lived openly with a man she loved, being refused the official release from a marriage of the same kind, which she hated. That was her crime—she loved, and I am my mother's son. It was something of a vengeance when I took the title, and I think my mother might be smiling in that little bit of heaven reserved for those who dare to take what the pagan gods offer them.'

'Are the pagan gods the only ones that you believe in, señor?' Toni spoke lightly, but there was an arrow tenseness to her body as he leaned against the wall beside her, a careless arrogance about him, the sea light upon his dark profile.

'I have to admit to a leaning towards them, Tonita. They seem to me less harsh towards the so-called sinners. What is sin? Does anyone really know? Joy-killers are looked upon as virtuous, and to kill joy is surely as nasty as taking a swipe at a butterfly and breaking its wing?'

'Joy in all that wine-green sea,' she asked, 'or in the wine glass? Joy in all that infinity of sky, or in a woman's eyes?'

He laughed softly. 'Don't you believe that I can find pleasure in simple things?'

'For a while, perhaps, but you like the saturnalia, and the gambling casinos, and driving very fast cars. I don't think you could ever settle down in Cornwall, or in Spain. You want to see everything—try as many things as possible. There is something in you that won't let you pause for too long.'

'The complete hedonist, eh?' His eyes brooded on the sea, whose surface glittered as if a million fish scales had been spilled upon it. He began to whistle very softly through his teeth, as if careless of anyone's opinion of him, least of all that of Toni. It was the wedding march ... mocking her for marrying him ... mocking the marriage itself, that would have no real meaning beyond that it suited his cynical mood to take a wife.

'The tide is so far out,' he said abruptly, 'but soon— all too soon it will turn and the sea will come crashing in over that line of rocks. Are you sure it won't disturb you to sleep within sound of all that pent-up fury?'

'I don't think it will,' she said. 'Will you be within hearing?'

He gave her a rather odd look when she said that, and instantly she realised that he thought she was being provocative. 'I mean, if I have a nightmare I'll have it under the bedcovers so you won't be disturbed.'

'Don't be a little fool, Toni! Haven't you learned yet that with me you don't have to suffer in silence?'

'But you said——' her eyes searched his face that was so like a baffling mask, always hiding the real man who was beyond her reach. 'You implied that if I had the sea tower, then I wasn't to—to be silly if the sound of the sea brought back that awful night when the *Miranda* went on the rocks.'

'*Dios*, do you have to take everything I say so much to heart?' He suddenly reached out and pulled her against the smooth material of his jacket, not gently but with a kind of roughness he might show a boy. Her heart gave a little trip, half with pleasure, half with pain. That was all she was to him, really, the gamine he had picked up off the floor of that noisy café, with the bewildering lights of the witch-ball playing over the scene. With that innate arrogance that wouldn't be challenged he had taken her aboard his yacht, and

117

when it had sunk and he had saved her, he had assumed this strange guardianship that had nothing to do with desire or love. She was his, as this house, this garden, that sandy cove were his. He took careless possession of her, unaware that she gave him all that she was.

'Dragging you out of the sea was probably the only virtuous thing I've done in a misspent life, Tonita. Anyway, we'll pass over my sins, for they aren't for the ears of innocence.' He gave a laugh that held a rather jarring sound. 'But what wouldn't I give to overhear some of the comments on our marriage—the devil's taken a bride, they'll say, and the odds are in favour of him breaking her heart.'

'It would have broken anyway, if I'd stayed behind those high walls that were shutting me away from—life,' she said. 'With you, *señor*, I'm alive until it hurts.'

'That's life, *chica*, a wild pleasure and a wilder pain. But how will you feel when people refer to you as the devil's bride?'

'I—I shall tell them all to go to hell.'

'You tell them that and they'll say I'm tutoring you in all the rude arts of the English tongue. You'll be my lady in all things, Toni, and a look of disdain will speak louder than any of the ungodly words you are likely to pick up from me.'

'Always supposing my temper doesn't get the better of me.' She drew back and gave him an impudent look. 'Even at the convent I could never quite control it, and Sister Imaculata always said that I was destined for the devil unless I learned humility.'

'It would seem that her prophecy came true! Humility, eh?' He grimaced at the word. 'The humble and the meek are trodden down, and that you won't be, with me! Come, our coffee was interrupted and I want several cups right now!'

CHAPTER EIGHT

THEY had coffee in the Chinese Room, where he lounged on the sofa while Toni wandered about the room looking at the paintings of pagodas and delicate bridges, admiring the beauty of the jade and ivory carvings, pausing to trace with her fingertips the panel figures of the lacquered cabinets.

It was a world of wonder and she was lost in it, but not so completely that she wasn't aware of Luque watching her from eyes narrowed and curious under his slanting eyelids.

'Their intrinsic beauty appeals to you and not the actual worth,' he said, and she smiled to herself as the combined scents of coffee and cheroot smoke drifted across the room to her.

She knelt beside a low Chinese table and fingered each oddment with a sense of delight which she couldn't have put into words. It was a delight which had its roots in several other things ... the sunlight through the curtains and across the surface of the carpet, the silky texture against her legs, warm and stroking ... as Luque's eyes stroked over her.

'I just like to touch them,' she said. 'I wouldn't wish to know how much they cost, for there's such a lot of hunger in the world that it seems almost criminal for little bits of jade and porcelain to cost more than food and shelter for poor people.'

'A laudable reaction, *chica*, but I do assure you that I provide big cheques for the poor, and you don't have to develop a conscience because very soon you will own these exotic baubles. They are there to be enjoyed.'

'I've never owned anything, except my own feelings,' she said, with a sense of wonder. And as she looked at Luque a thrill of fear and excitement ran through her ... soon he would own her and then he might see her in a different light, if she grew a little more bosom and wore some of that lilac shadow on her eyes, like Birdina.

'Do you like women who wear make-up?' she asked him suddenly.

'If they wear it correctly and not like clowns. But if you're making plans to get yourself up like Birdina, then drop them. Birdy was made in pastels and she can take the paint, but you'd look a sort of jester.'

'*Gracias, señor!* You pay me some pretty compliments!'

'Are you hungry for some flattery, you skinny brat?' His eyes held arrant mockery as they passed over her. 'Hair cut under a basin, and eyes like two spoonfuls of green honey—what would you have me say, your ladyship?'

'Well, you might pretend that I—I'm attractive. After all, you are marrying me, for what it's worth.'

'Yes, for what it's worth.' He lifted his cheroot and blew a perfect smoke ring in her direction, as if to indicate that her wedding ring would be as intangible to him as smoke in the air. 'The term "attractive" can cover anything from a bed of tulips to a seaside resort, and I prefer specific terms of reference. Right now you're a graceless adolescent with legs all over the place, and hips and elbows with corners to them. One day—maybe—you'll be a bit of a witch and then I shall ask an artist friend of mine to paint your portrait.'

'Oh, have you friends?' she said impudently. 'I thought the devil only had idolisers.'

'You're asking for trouble with that kind of talk, pup!'

'Am I, *señor hidalgo*?'

'A cuffing, and don't think I wouldn't provide it.'

'I'm sure you'd never hesitate to discipline your *peons*.'

'That is what you are, eh?'

'Much more that,' she gave a defiant laugh, 'than any ladyship.'

'So Aunt Charlotte and Birdina did get under your skin, eh?'

'I'd have to be covered in cowhide not to have felt a few pricks. Your aunt is right, where are my social graces and my poise? You have just told me that I'm a gawky thing with corners, and it's perfectly true that you're marrying me to get back at the Helburns. Your idea of a twisted joke, and after a time jokes aren't all that funny. They become tedious, and that is one thing you like to avoid.'

'I see, Tonita. You've been scratched and you need to be reassured that there's no real venom left in the wounds. Come over here to me, for I'm feeling too comfortable to move.' He clicked his fingers. 'Come on!'

'I'm comfortable myself, and I can lick my own wounds,' she said, bending over the table and picking up a lacquered bowl. 'What a pretty thing, as delicate as spun-glass.'

'Put that down and come over here,' he ordered.

She cast him a mutinous look, her long lashes quivering across her grey-green eyes. 'Why should I?' she asked.

'*Peons* don't question the orders flung at them,' he said, stubbing his cheroot in an ashtray on the sofa table. 'Do as you're told.'

At first there had been a taunting laziness in his manner, but now his face and voice had altered and Toni felt a tightening of her nerves, a slight tremor in her fingers so that as she replaced the bowl it slid on the smooth surface of the table and fell to the floor. 'Oh no!' Fear clutched at her, for she thought the lovely thing had broken and she hardly dared to pick it up.

'Don't faint,' Luque mocked her. 'If it's broken, then we can get a tube of glue and stick it together again.'

'Its beauty would be spoilt,' her fingers stroked it. 'It isn't harmed, thank goodness.'

'Then put it down before there's a real accident and I have to move off this sofa in order to fetch the *sal volatile*.'

'You mock everything,' she muttered. 'People—things—I suppose because you can replace them so easily.'

'Or glue them together.' He reached out a lean hand and pulled her downwards, on to his hard chest under the shirt of grey-striped silk. Toni felt the quick warmth of him, and her own inability to resist her feelings with regard to him. He infuriated her, and yet she loved him. She fought with him, but she never really won any of their battles. He was devil and idol all in one. He could make her smile, and make her cry, just as he willed.

She stared down into his taunting eyes and wished she were an enchantress with red lips and a thousand wiles—how she would make *him* suffer!

'I'm not a bit comfortable like this—it was softer on the carpet.'

'Too bad.' He drew her closer, pressing her slim body all down the length of his, holding her inescapably, when there came a discreet tap at the door.

Lanyon entered and politely informed Luque he had been to the station and brought back the packages from London.

'Good man,' said Luque. 'Take them up to Miss Fleet's bedroom and we'll open them in a while.'

'Very good, my lord. Shall I remove the coffee tray?'

Luque nodded, and Toni was intensely aware of his arms holding her locked to him, an embrace which must look very suggestive to an observer.

'My aunt and her daughter got away all right, Lanyon?' As Luque spoke his eyes were upon Toni's face, arrantly aware of her discomfiture.

'Yes, sir. They are now on their way back to London.'

'Thank heaven,' said Luque, with a disgraceful lack of family feeling.

'Will that be all, my lord?'

'Yes, Lanyon, Tell Tamsin that we'll be dining at home tonight, and we'll have a bottle of the Château d'Or with our dinner.'

'As you wish, my lord.' The door closed behind the imperturbable figure of Luque's butler, and Toni could only suppose that so often had he seen his master with a woman in his arms that it no longer surprised or shocked him.

'I can feel you blushing right through your dress,' Luque drawled. 'Don't you like being this close to me?'

'It's something I—I'm not used to——'

'I should hope not! But you were feeling a bit clawed and you needed to have your mind taken off dear Aunt Charlotte's visit. A man has two certain ways of distracting a woman, he takes her to the dress shop, or he takes her in his arms. Well, my funny one, are you sufficiently distracted?'

'Yes—you know a fearful lot about women, *señor*.'

She glanced away from his eyes that seemed to know all the secrets of the female psyche.

'Enough, but not quite everything.' His hand curved about the nape of her neck and slowly and deliberately he pulled her face down to his and she felt his lips brush warm and smoky across hers. 'Some fine, inexplicable thread vibrates between us. Tonita, as if in another existence we shared a certain experience. I wonder what it was, eh? Tell me, do you believe in reincarnation?'

'I—I've never really thought about it,' she said shakily.

'It's a fascinating idea, that aeons ago we might have met in another life. Does your spirit feel linked to mine?'

It was her body that felt itself a part of him, superimposed as it was upon the masculine length of him so that she felt his breathing and the warm beating of the veins beneath his brown skin.

'Knowing me in this life is enough for you, eh? Do you think me a very bad man, Tonita?'

'I wouldn't like you for an enemy,' she said. 'Birdina told me that you once broke a man's arm.'

'So Birdy tried to scare you off me—did she succeed?'

'It would hardly seem so! I know you can be ruthless, señor. It's in your face—I saw it there when your Aunt Charlotte turned up. I always thought that having a family must be—oh, I don't know, a sort of security against being alone.'

'I daresay there are families that enjoy a real and abiding relationship, chica, so don't judge the Helburns by decent standards. We're an arrogant, self-willed clan, and I have the added disadvantage of being half Spanish. A Spaniard is either a saint or a devil, or a high-class waiter, and you know what I am, don't you!'

'You're Luque, and you fed me and didn't preach.'
A painful thickness came into Toni's throat, and she
thought of what Birdina had said, that sometimes
Luque could make a girl feel like crying. Impulsively
Toni kissed him, meaning to pull away instantly, but
he held her to him and this time he took her offered
lips with a sudden savagery, and somehow, in some
mysterious way that she was hardly aware of, he
changed their positions so that she lay beneath him,
pressed into the cushions, at the mercy of his lean,
hard, raking strength. This was Luque, and she was
unafraid, as in the strangest way she had been unafraid
when she had plunged with him into the stormy sea
and a similar breathless feeling had swept over her ...

The shock came when, his lips warm and seeking
at her throat, he suddenly wrenched away from her
and left her alone on the sofa. He stood there, staring
down at her, the shirt pulled away from a hammering
pulse at his own throat.

'Don't you ever,' he said grimly, 'let any other man
behave like that with you! I should be whipped, not
that it had much effect years ago when my own father
took his riding-switch to me. Ironical that he should
be incensed by *his* son's behaviour with one of the
grape-pickers! But you're no flirtatious grape-picker
with plenty of experience of men and their ways, so
you can sit up and pull your dress down over your
knees!'

Toni did so, and she could feel herself shaking at
the dark look on his face. It was as if he had carried
her off to a strange heaven, only to fling her down to
earth with a painful thump. Their eyes quarrelled
violently as he stood there, frowning down at her, and
then she turned her head away and swore to herself
that she wasn't on the verge of tears.

But he knew, as he seemed to know a lot of tormenting things. 'For the love of heaven don't cry,' he said, in that voice that was clipped and almost foreign. 'We all have lessons to learn, and now you know how foolhardy it can be to offer your lips to a man. Almost as foolish as taking a swim in a high tide, when you can be swept out into deeps from which there's no escape once they get out of control. Men, my little nun, can very easily get out of control, so you remember it and keep your kisses to yourself.'

'D-don't worry, Luque, I shall never kiss you again —never.' The tears were stinging her eyelids, and the pain was hard and hurting in her throat. She wanted to rush out of sight of him, to hide away, and not have to speak to this cruel stranger into which Luque had changed. 'I hate you!' She jumped to her feet and the movement shook the tears from her eyes. 'You're like everyone else—I live on your charity and that makes me a good target when you want to lash out. You haven't any real affection in you—not one scrap—and I don't want to stay with you!'

With these words she began to wrench at the diamond ring on her left hand ... and then she cried out as his hand swept down and gripped her to stillness. 'It's better to hate me, Toni, for I can hurt you less if you hate me. Do you understand?'

'No,' she said, struggling to release her hands from his. 'I thought men married women because they—they liked them. I wanted to like you, but you only want me as a sort of shadow in your life. Someone amenable to your moods, who has to be grateful for the clothes you choose her to wear, and the food you give her to eat. I—I might as well be one of those *papier mâché* figures in the window of a shop!'

'If only you were,' he mocked, 'for you talk too much. Don't you like the clothes I give you?'

'They're all right.' She shrugged her shoulders, indifferently. 'As you told Birdina, I'm quite happy in a pair of jeans and a shirt. I've never been used to much —this ring, for instance, is a bit much. No wonder your Aunt Charlotte looked at me askance. Whoever heard of a nobody dressed up in a diamond ring!'

'Stop it, Toni,' he warned.

'Sorry, *señor master*, but I can't stop breathing and become a *papier mâché* image that can't think, feel, or cry.' She had begun to tremble, for she wasn't a paper doll and she couldn't hate him as easily as she could say the words. He had hold of her heart even if he didn't want it; he had control of her life even as she fought him.

'To hell with this!' He suddenly pulled her against his shoulder and pressed his hand to the back of her head, pushing his fingers into her ruffled red hair. 'I can't just let you out into the world, so that you can give your hungry little heart to the next rotter who comes along. Nor can I take you eternally sailing as my cabin-boy. I can only make you my wife, Tonita, for it has got around that you've been with me and there are those who will take advantage of your ineffable inexperience and your guileless honesty. Come and see your wedding dress!'

She wanted to refuse him, but the fight had run out of her and very quietly she went with him across the hall and up a flight of carved stairs, along a gallery and up some more stairs that twined in a spiral to the door of the sea tower.

They entered an apartment that at any other time would have struck her as delightful, for she saw deep window alcoves, a love-seat cushioned in red velvet, and some foreign-looking furniture painted with fish and flowers. Luque walked through this circular-walled room into another, where on a bed with tall posts and a blue brocade cover there were the mixture of boxes

127

from London. Toni watched as he ripped off the wrapping-paper and lifted lids, scattering them across the bed and beckoning her to come and look.

Toni hesitated, for it wasn't too easily forgotten that downstairs they had shared a scene which had ripped at her feelings and left her in a depressed mood. She wasn't to be won over by presents, for she wasn't a child.

'Don't sulk,' he said. 'That won't be the first of our rows, or the last, and I can't abide a sulky female.'

'I'm not sulking,' she denied, and it was true. The things they had said to each other had struck deeper than that; he seemed not to understand that she wanted to do her share of the giving, and all she had to give was herself.

'Birdina said that it's unlucky for the—the bridegroom to see the bride's dress before the actual day of the wedding.'

'Sheer superstitious rot, Tonita.' He lifted a fragile silken garment out of one of the boxes and studied it, a quirk to his eyebrow. 'It's a mystery to me that women don't go around in a perpetual state of fever— or perhaps they do! Pretty thing, isn't it? I suppose it's what you call a slip—H'm, a Freudian slip, I shouldn't wonder.'

Toni knew that he was trying to charm her out of her fit of the blues, and instead she wanted to grab things off the dressing-table and aim them at his arrogant head. Oh God, what kind of a marriage was it going to be when he chose not to treat her as a woman? That was what she wanted! To be his—to belong to him utterly, from her heart to her heels!

'I chose to have your dress made in London for two reasons,' he said, lounging against one of the bedposts and regarding her from under half-lowered eyelids.

'The dressmaker is a good one, and you aren't accustomed yet to dealing with such people.'

'You mean that I'm a naïve girl from a convent who hasn't yet developed a taste in the kind of clothes worn by people of your class,' she said. 'I might select the wrong material and the wrong style, and it's bad enough that Lord Helburn is marrying a little nobody.'

'Toni, *mia*,' he mocked, 'it isn't like you to be a little bore. That was one of the things I liked about you on the *Miranda*, you amused me and didn't moon about with the usual female blues. I thought that a kind of miracle, from someone who had spent half her life washing up other people's messy dishes and scrubbing dirty floors. What has come over you?'

'I—I suppose I'm nervous,' she said, but that wasn't the real truth. Love had come over her and she wanted to run to him and have him pull her hard and close into his arms, as wanting of her as she was of him. But it was something she couldn't do ... he didn't want her kisses.

'Yes, it's quite a step for both of us to be taking, and you're very young, very untried.' A smile quirked the edge of his mouth. 'But for all that, surely you're curious about your wedding dress?'

As his voice softened and the mockery left his eyes, Toni went to him and was shown the box in which the dress was concealed by tissue-paper. With hands that trembled she folded back the soft white paper and caught her breath as the dress was revealed. Wordlessly she lifted it out of the box and gave a shiver as the delicate material brushed her skin ... the style was a very simple one, but she knew instinctively that it was right for her and she couldn't help but fall in love with a colour that was like jade held to the light so that it shimmered a silvery green.

'Did you choose the colour?' she asked Luque breath-lessly.

He nodded, reaching out a hand to a diaphanous sleeve, his lean fingers dark against the chiffon-silk. 'Does it meet with your ladyship's approval?'

'Oh yes,' colour ran over her cheekbones, for when he touched the dress it was as if he touched her. 'Every-thing about the dress is just lovely, and I—I only wish I wasn't so funny and gawky, for I shall never do it justice.'

'You think not?' He looked into her eyes, and his own eyes were lash-shadowed and enigmatic. 'We'll see, my witch. Now take a look at the rest of the trousseau and keep yourself amused while I go and make a tele-phone call.'

He strolled from the bedroom and a moment later the door of the outer room closed behind him and Toni was left alone, surrounded by boxes in which lay lovely things *just for her*. Was this how Cinderella had felt when the magic wand had been waved, changing her from a kitchen drudge into the captivator of a prince?

Toni's smile was shaky on her lips, and she felt the melting away of that cold, hurt feeling. She pressed to her face the dress of softest chiffon, lovely and lis-som as sea-water and shadows. It was no use, she was caught for good or bad in the mystifying charm of the man, as if she were a moth fascinated by a flame. Her inner torment was subtle, but it could be borne, and not just because he bought her the kind of things that every girl's heart hungered for. He was Luque and that was enough, and even if she ever really hated him, she would still love him more.

The rest of her bridal outfit consisted of pretty jade-green shoes, gloves and bag to match the shoes, and a little hat that made her look like Mercury ... the gods' messenger.

She stared at herself in the mirror, and then felt her nerves tighten as a small clock chimed on the table beside the bed. It came as a surprise that it was now late in the afternoon. She glanced across at the windows and saw the fading gold of the sky, the stretching shadows, the quiver of redness on the windowpanes.

Still wearing the Mercury hat, she approached one of the casements and opened it to the voice of the sea and the darkening air filled with a salty spray. She could hear the waves on the rocks as she leaned there in the honeycomb of mullioned windowpanes, breathing the cool and dusky scents as the sun began to die away.

The sound and the scents of the sea wafted her back to the *Miranda* and those evenings on her deck, and Toni could hardly bear to think that the lovely yacht now lay mangled by the rocks, being slowly battered into so much driftwood. Luque had said in the car coming here that he wouldn't permit salvage of the *Miranda*; like the good sailor she had always been, she was buried at sea.

Toni wondered if she would sail with Luque on his new yacht, or would he leave her behind at Mawgan Plas? Whatever he decided she would accept as part of the bargain ... it seemed possible to love this old house in the wilds of Cornwall, where his mother had found the happiness denied to her in Spain.

How far away from the *plas* was the convent, with its strict rules, its vesper bells, and high walls shutting girls like her away from men like Luque.

And yet here she was, only days away from becoming his bride ... bride of the devil, he had said, and Toni shivered as she remembered that she had been

131

meant for a far different bridal. One that embraced an ideal and not the vital aliveness of a man whose skin had felt so warm and taut against her own.

Was she a heathen? Sister Imaculata had said it sometimes, when she was extra annoyed with Toni for gossiping with the garden boy or chewing the carrots like a hungry rabbit. Toni caught her breath in a half frightened, half amused sob. Whatever she was, she had not been fashioned for the grey habit and the path of virtue. To avoid them she had risked breaking her neck, and she would do it again, if some terrible mischance separated her from Luque and she found herself back behind those stony walls.

'I suppose I'm like my mother,' she murmured to herself. 'I have to give all for the sake of what I feel for a man, and if that makes me a heathen, then I suppose I am one.'

She drew away from the window and found that the bedroom of the sea tower had darkened around her. She found her way to the light switch and blinked as the walls and furnishings sprang into brightness around her.

That tall-posted bed with the billowy eiderdown was hers to sleep in ... all hers, taking up as much space as four of the convent beds had taken up. There were basket chairs with rose-red cushions, delicate rose-painted bowls on the dressing-table, and underfoot a thick creamy carpet with massive roses worked into it, and big curly green leaves.

'I hope, miss, that you find things to your satisfaction?'

Toni's nerves gave a jump she swung round to find a woman by the bedroom door, staring at her with eyes as dark as those of a Spanish nun. Even her dress was dark, and the hair that was drawn back from a face that had a look of sadness stamped into it. She was like some of those women in Spain, who after the loss of someone they loved took to wearing dark colours, and who even walked on the sombre side of the road out of the sunlight. They became withdrawn, a little harsh, as if their grief made them a little mad.

CHAPTER NINE

'THE room is very nice, thank you.' Toni stood there nervously, while the dark eyes roved over her, making a silent assessment of her, from her ruffled red hair down to the feet from which she had kicked the high-heeled shoes.

'I am Tamsin. I saw to these rooms and as Lord Helburn said you were only a girl, I thought you'd like the blue and rose colours.'

'I like them very much, but I'm afraid I've made the bedroom terribly untidy with my unpacking.'

'It will take no time at all to clear up, miss.' With these words Tamsin came to the bed and began to collect together the littered sheets of tissue-paper. At the same time her eyes were upon the pretty, delicate garments which Toni had taken from the boxes. 'His lordship is a generous man, miss.'

'Yes.' Toni flushed, for something in the woman's manner had made her seem one of those girls who wheedled gifts out of a man. 'All my belongings were lost in the wreck of the *Miranda* and Luque—Lord Helburn was good enough to replace them.'

'Of course, miss.' But as Tamsin fingered a fine silk slip it was obvious what she was thinking, that never in her life before had Toni possessed lingerie from one of the best shops in London, nor dresses designed by a master, and shoes which had been hand-lasted. Toni wondered just how much Tamsin knew, and how much she surmised about the girl who come next

Friday would be mistress of Mawgan Plas.

'I hope, Tamsin, that we shall get along all right. I'm not used to this kind of life, as you've probably guessed.'

'Yes, miss.' The dark eyes were intent upon Toni's face. 'His lordship explained that you were in a convent—in Spain. Many years ago I used to live there myself. I went there with Madam, his lordship's mother, to be her personal maid when her family arranged her marriage to the Don Beltran de Mayo y Juanluis. When Madam left San Luis Bara and came here to Cornwall, I came with her. I have known his lordship from a baby, miss.'

'Have you, Tamsin?' Toni saw it all in those few words of explanation—the young maid devoted to the girl who had obeyed her family and gone to Spain to marry a man she neither loved, nor was loved by. That deep devotion extended to Luque, and no one, least of all a naïve girl like Toni, would ever find complete favour in the eyes of Tamsin.

'His lordship's mother was one of the loveliest girls in London that season of her marriage.' Tamsin looked at Toni with a flicker of barely concealed scorn in her eyes. 'She had truly golden hair, you know, and eyes of a gold-amber colour. At her presentation at the palace she wore a dress that I remember to this day, a shift of pale silk with a tunic of sheer lilac. She had her portrait painted in the dress and she wore a small tiara of diamonds; a photograph of the portrait appeared in a foreign magazine and that was how Don Beltran came to—want her. It was not a happy union, miss. Two people who aren't suited in ways and temperament should never become man and wife, for it only leads to a great deal of misery. Private misery at first, and then the kind that involves other people—especially the children, if there are any. His lordship had to be left in Spain when his mother left, for she knew how much turmoil and trouble there would be if she took Don Beltran's son away from him—but that's how it should have been! The boy would have been happy here at Mawgan Plas——'

Tamsin broke off and bit her lip. She had lifted the lid off private thoughts and old hurts which had probably been simmering ever since Luque had told her of his forthcoming marriage. She believed that Toni was the wrong kind of wife for him, and she saw history repeating itself!

Toni's own doubts and fears came to the surface ... she thought of the dark, passionate anger with which he had flung her away from him, down there in the Chinese Room. He had been brought up by a bitter, unloving man, and taught by his mother's defection that love was not to be trusted.

He wanted a marriage in which love would play no part, but Toni had been denied love for so long that she knew it would break her heart if she wasn't loved. She knew this, and she had to believe that it could be borne.

'I shall do my best to make Luque happy,' she said. 'I shall try to be the kind of wife that he wants.'

'That is what Madam said when she married his father. I was with her, in her room brushing her beautiful hair, the night before we made the journey to San Luis Bara. She believed that living there would compensate her for—other things. But it never did!'

'You can't believe that I'm marrying Luque because I want to possess all this?' Toni swept her hand around the sea tower and gestured towards the windows. 'It wouldn't matter to me if he had nothing but a fishing boat and earned his living catching shrimps. I—I'm not that kind of a person!'

'You're very young, miss. You may not know your

own mind as yet.'

'I know my heart!' The words broke from Toni and her eyes were passionate with anger. 'How dare you speak to me as if I'm some kind of an opportunist—it's unfair! Everyone seems to assume that my marriage is doomed before it begins.'

'Perhaps it is doomed—many things are.' Tamsin ran a hand over the silk eiderdown covering the big bed, smoothing away the creases. She carried the lingerie to the chest and laid it away in the deep drawers. Then she picked up the shimmering jade-green dress in which Toni was to be married, and Toni just about stopped herself from leaping forward and snatching it away from the woman.

'If you were a daughter of mine, miss, I'd advise you to find another man, or another life for yourself. His lordship can be kind enough, but he's a strange one— it's the mixed blood in him, and the unhappiness as a boy, being parted from his mother and being brought up to believe her a wanton.'

Toni shuddered at the word, which was so cruel and graphic.

'Someone has to make up for all that,' she said. 'I'm going to try——'

'You, miss?' Tamsin turned from the wardrobe where she had hung the bright dress away in the darkness. 'Beautiful women have tried to make him happy, and no doubt you'll be seeing some of them, for they like the high life as he does. He'll never settle down to country life, you know. Coming home to Mawgan Plas for a couple of weeks each year is about all he can endure of the quietness and the simple way of things. You can take it from me, miss, no bit of a girl like yourself is going to change his lordship's way of living.'

'I wouldn't dream of trying,' Toni protested. 'Luque is his own master——'

'As well you know, miss. I expect that's why he's marrying the likes of you—so you won't get in his way.'

'How very unkind you are—all of you!' Toni could feel herself trembling, and her anger had given way to a cold, creeping despair. 'If I were a superficial society beauty, with a heart as hard as a diamond, you'd all be pleased—as if all Luque is worth is a woman who lives only for pleasure.'

'That is what the half-gods live for, miss. "Sin and success and pleasure. And the hideous image of Gold." In marriage like unto like should come together, and you're not his sort.'

'What sort am I?' Toni asked, defiantly. 'I was with him on the yacht and everyone assumed that I had been his—mistress.'

'The newspaper reporters might have assumed it, but his lordship wouldn't be marrying you if you'd been as easy to win as a hand of cards. I'm wondering, miss, if there's some special favourite you would like for dessert this evening? Perhaps apricots *à la Parisienne*, the fruits being halved and poached in a vanilla syrup, the two halves then filled with cream and rejoined?'

'Th—the sweet sounds very appetizing. Yes, I should like that.'

'Very well, miss——'

'Please, can't any of you say something kind about my marriage?' Toni pleaded. 'You were close to his mother—you must wish him a little happiness?'

'What is happiness?' Tamsin gazed at Toni with blank, dark eyes, in which not a ray of light seemed to show. 'My dear Madam had to give up her child in order to find it, and I believed I had found it when I had my own son. But it never does to bet on happiness, miss. You can have it one minute, right there in your heart, and the next minute it has flown away never to

138

return. Don't bet on happiness, or on love. It's a charm —and a curse!'

The bedroom door closed on Toni, who sank down on the bed and stared at the woven roses and leaves of the carpet. The room was warm, for there were radiators at either end of it, but she felt cold ... as cold as she had sometimes felt at the convent when the winter winds blew down from the mountains ... those high shining peaks that the sun never seemed to melt.

She had fled from the convent, and now she wondered if she should run away from Mawgan Plas, now while it was dark, before she saw Luque again.

They were two different people from different ends of the earth ... she had a heart to break, while his was like those imperial peaks, untouchable and invulnerable. Beautiful women who belonged to his world had failed to win his heart, so what hope had she? Tamsin was right. She should try and find another kind of life for herself ... she had her health and her vitality and hard work had never worried her. If she kept herself she kept her pride ... there was nothing to be proud of in being a wife in name only.

Oh God, she felt so cold, from her feet upwards. Cold like the diamond on her hand, whose fire seemed a frozen thing. Downstairs he had stopped her from removing the ring, but now she was alone it came off easily, glittering as she held it, like a small star fallen from the heaven it had seemed at first, when he had said that she might stay and marry him.

She placed it on the bedside table and then went across to the bathroom that adjoined her bedroom. She tried the water and found it hot and steaming. Yes, that was what she needed, a hot bath that would warm the chill from her bones and relax her nerves. Common sense told her that she couldn't leave the *plas* till the morning, for coming here Luque had talked of the

139

moors and the sandy bogs, and Cornwall seemed more menacing in some respects than the Spain she had known from a child.

She took off her dress and the silky underthings that were so luxurious after the plain and rather itchy undergarments that she had worn at the convent. She ran her fingers down the slip and they tingled at the contact ... flesh against silk, exciting and forbidden ... as it had been forbidden to see one's own body in a mirror. Now she looked at herself in the half-steamy mirror on the wall of the bathroom and she thought of what Luque had said about her gawky legs and her boyish hips.

If only she had a curving and seductive body ... oh, drat such thoughts, and she sat down clumsily in the bath and scattered water all over the marbled floor. Taking hold of the loofah and the soap she began to scrub some warmth back into her limbs ... life was much easier for people who didn't ask questions of it and just accepted whatever came along, but Toni knew she would never be one of these. She wasn't naturally passive, and that was why she had caused Sister Imaculata so much concern.

Stretching a well-lathered leg, Toni wondered what had been the reaction when the good Sister had found that her rebel had gone over the wall to freedom. They would have looked for her, but by then she was on board Luque's yacht and he had set the course for her.

A stormy one which had brought her to this house of a wizard ... love is a charm and a curse, Tamsin had said, and as cold fingers seemed to run across Toni's bare wet shoulders she plunged down into the water, burying herself in the soapy warmth, wishing that all thought could stop and she could pretend that everything was all right.

Deep in the water of the big deep bath she felt

drowsy, and let her eyes steal around the blue and white tiled walls and rest on the large fluffy towels that lay in readiness over the heated rail. The luxury of everything was still very strange to her ... if she were a mercenary girl, with a heart that could be content with luxury, she would shrug off the doubts and fears and plunge headlong into the enjoyment of lovely things to wear, good food to eat, and a great silky bed to sleep in ... all to herself.

Why ... oh, why did she have to feel these tormenting doubts? But she knew why ... it was because his Aunt Charlotte was right, and Birdina, and that strange woman in grieving clothes. She wasn't the right woman for Luque. She knew nothing of his world, and she had nothing to give him that he wanted. When he had kissed her, it had not been with tenderness but with a cynical savagery, as if to warn her that a ravishment was not a loving.

With a sigh Toni took hold of the chromium handles of the bath and pulled herself to her feet, the water streaming down her body. There was a shower nozzle overhead and she turned it, gasping as the cool water needled down on her skin and washed off the soap. She was tingling all over as she hopped from the bath ... and then she was crying out as her feet slid on the wet floor and a sickening pain flared all through her as her elbow struck the solid side of the bath.

She went down in a heap and was dazedly aware of the bathroom door being thrust open, and she heard footfalls on the tiled floor as she sat there nursing her arm, tears of pain in her eyes.

'Demonio, what is this? What have you done?' Someone was bending over her, lifting her, and she gave a little sob as her elbow was jarred.

'You are wet as a fish and white as a sheet—where have you struck yourself?'

141

'M-my elbow,' she said shakily. 'It hurts like hell!'

'I can see that it does, and don't use bad language just because I do. Come, let us have a look at the damage.' As he strode with her from the bathroom he snatched a towel from the rail, and it wasn't until he sat her down on the bed and began to wrap the towel around her that Toni realised her nakedness. She shook back her wet hair with a gesture of distress and looked up into eyes that were concerned and seemed unaware of handling a bare female body.

He took her left arm into his fingers and ran them across her elbow, already marked by a red welt. 'I'm going to press the bone,' he warned her. 'You may only have bruised it, but we have to make sure. Your young bones aren't all that well padded and you could have cracked one of them. Hold on, *chica*.'

He pressed and the room swam and Toni felt sick. Her elbow hurt so much that it frightened her, and then a quiver ran all through her as Luque stroked the wet hair away from her eyes. 'It's badly bruised, and I'm going to fetch an ice-pack and a drop of brandy. Lie back on the bed, Tonita. I shan't be more than a few minutes.'

She lay as he left her and she thought dismally that she must be the most tiresome and unexciting fiancée that a man ever had. A tear or two trickled down the side of her nose, and she felt the throbbing pain as not quite so acute now. Thank goodness! It would have made things awkward if she had had to run away from Mawgan Plas with her arm in a sling. Washing-up jobs weren't available for the incapacitated ... in fact there were very few jobs that one could tackle with a cracked bone.

'Come, sit up for me and drink this.' A strong arm snaked around her and she gave herself to Luque's ministrations. The brandy was warm and strong and it

142

made her think of that night on the *Miranda*, when she had believed that he thought her a boy. She sipped the brandy and felt him very close to her on the bed ... as if Luque could ever be fooled by any female, young or old. His eyes as they dwelt on her face seemed to hold a hundred inscrutable secrets. He knew all about women, and bones, and how to keep a cool head in any emergency. He was so adult, and she was so immature that he could look upon her nudity as he might look upon an infant playing wet and bare on a beach.

With the brandy inside her, and the ice-pack pressed against her elbow, she soon felt very much better. 'Th-thank you, Luque, for being kind,' she said. 'You always seem to be coming to my rescue——'

'Your knight in black armour, eh?' He went into the bathroom and returned with a fresh towel, all warm from the heated rail. 'Come, my damsel in distress, you need a rub down, for I don't want you laid up with a cold and I don't want you sniffling and sneezing at the altar next Friday.'

'I—I'm not going to marry you, Luque.' Even as she spoke the words she could feel the pressure of his hands through the towel and the overwhelming intimacy of what was happening here in her bedroom. He was drying her slim whiteness, and she wasn't an infant on a beach but a grown girl with feelings which responded to his touch.

'Really?' he said, and he held the orange towel so that it was bright against her white shoulders. 'That needle is still stuck in the groove, is it? That tune is still playing? It grows tedious.'

'I—I'm the tedious one, *señor*. I'm awkward, naïve and hopeless, and Tamsin was right when she said that like should marry like.'

'So you have met Tamsin, eh? And she has taken it upon herself to cast her stone at us. My dear Tonita, it

143

couldn't be expected of that poor woman to see anything but the shadows; to hear anything but her own cries when she went looking for her small son and found only his bucket and spade by a rock-pool. She's the wife of my gamekeeper. She was the mother of the little boy I told you about ... the one who vanished into a beach bog.'

'Oh no!' Toni gripped his shoulder with her right hand and recalled the terrible aura of grief which had hung about Tamsin. 'Oh, Luque, I never realised—I thought her sadness was connected with your mother, for she mentioned being her maid. How awful, to send a child out to play and never to see him again. Oh, what a travail for her. A pain that can never end.'

'Unfortunately a pain that can't be eased.' With these words he took Toni's elbow very carefully in his fingers and her heart turned over as he bent his head and laid his lips against the bruise that was darkening on her skin.

'This is feeling a little easier?' he asked her. '*Dios*, but you are going to have a bruise of many colours. How did you fall?'

'I splashed about a bit and the floor was wet. It was my own fault——' Toni was trembling, for his kiss had gone right through her, as if it were the caress of a lover instead of being the kind of kiss that an infant received on a bumped portion of its anatomy.

'It must make quite a change, *chica*, for you to splash about in a big marble tub after those donkey troughs at the convent.'

'Yes.' Her smile was shaky. 'Everything at Mawgan Plas is lovely, and I wish I didn't feel guilty about them. But I'm not a suitable person for you to marry.'

'How very Victorian,' he mocked. 'You're free, white and virginal, aren't you? A trio of very suitable requisites, my funny child. And why the devil you should feel guilty about the enjoyment of nice things is a mystery to me. Explain yourself.'

'I—I haven't earned them,' she said. 'You're offering them to me, and I'm not expected to give you anything.'

'What would you like to give, Tonita?'

She lowered her gaze from his, for she knew that what she offered him lay in her eyes, and she had already been through the trauma of being rejected by him.

'I wish I could give you poise and knowledge, and all the things you are used to in the women you have —loved.'

'Loved?' he echoed, and the irony was back in his eyes as he tilted her chin with one hand, and held the towel around her with the other hand. Not too securely, for Toni could feel it slipping and she saw his lips quirk as she twitched the towel back in place.

'What gives you the idea that I have ever loved?' he asked, a taunting note in his voice. 'I've had affairs, for let's face it, *chica*, I am double your age, and I'm my father's son. But what has that kind of thing to do with love?'

'I wouldn't know,' she said, colour rising in her face.

'Do you imagine that a man loves every woman who falls into his arms? He'd end up with a harem if that were the case.'

'I know you're getting a rise out of me, Luque. Didn't I just say that I have no knowledge of your world and can only be a joke among your friends if we go through with our impossible marriage?'

'To the devil with friends—what friends?' Abruptly he gripped the ends of the towel and drew Toni's slim, barely covered shape up against his chest. 'You, you sprat, I *own*. You're my object, my person ... mine to gift, or taunt, or whip, do you hear? My bit of flotsam

145

from the sea, white as sun-scoured driftwood and green as wild honey. I've owned many things in my time, but never a bit of a girl, and I'm not giving you up no matter how much you struggle. We'll have no more of this nonsense about not marrying me. It's the only way I can keep you with me without causing another Helburn scandal—much as I'd personally enjoy the fun. But you're sensitive, hurtable, and my soul isn't yet as black as Paddy's sow.

'Well,' he brushed at her tousled hair, 'do I have your promise that you won't have another attack of the jitters about next Friday?'

Toni lay very still against him and she felt overwhelmed by her inability to escape this man, whose sardonic whim it was that she be his object; his to gift, taunt, or whip.

'I feel like a moth on a pin,' she murmured. 'You have me no matter how I struggle.'

'Quite so, *chica*. I have you!' He gave a brief laugh and she felt his warm breath against her temple. 'When you slipped over that convent wall you left the safety of the saints behind you and ran headlong into the devil's arms. So be it!'

'So be it,' she echoed, and closing her eyes she felt him lay her back against a pillow and wrap her in the silk eiderdown. Then he left her alone and the light clicked out.

She slept for about an hour and awoke feeling hungry, bruised, but a lot braver. She rose and dressed herself in one of the new dresses, which had a soft cowl collar and long sleeves which concealed the many-hued bruise all around her elbow. She combed her hair into a gleaming red cap, and replaced the diamond ring on her left hand. Love and Luque had defeated her, and she went downstairs to him, a slender, page-like figure against the gleaming dark wood of the staircase.

She saw the figure of Kwan Yin gleaming in the hooded wall-lighting and she hoped that Luque would have asked Lanyon to serve dinner in the Chinese Room. The dining-room was probably very grand, and he knew that he had to give her time to get used to the more formal aspects of being his lady.

Yes, he was there, standing tall and very still against a silk screen with embroidered birds flying wing to wing. He smiled as she entered the room and held out a hand to her. There were ebony studs on the ice-white cuffs of his dress shirt. His dinner jacket, black tie and trousers were impeccable, yet instead of looking starched he gave an impression of being alive and supple as an animal in its sleek skin.

'I knew you would be a brave girl and come down to me,' he said, his fingers gripping hers. 'I'm pleased. Tamsin has made us a very special dinner, I am informed by Lanyon. We are to have apricots *à la Parisienne* because I used to like them as a boy. Mm, I like that dress.'

'You bought it,' she reminded him, and had to force herself not to shy away when he leaned forward and sniffed her skin.

'Perfume as well, eh? Very enticing.'

'You bought that as well, *señor*. I wouldn't know an enticing perfume from a dab of cologne.'

'What I actually did, *chica*, was to give orders to the people at Justine St. Cyr. She's young, I told them, rather like a Titian boy, with eyes that go from jade to grey. I must say they know their business, and now will you accept this without having a spell of guilt because someone should spend a pound on you instead of donating it to the restoration of a steeple or a font? Now don't look like that—I warned you I was godless.'

'You're really terrible, *señor*,' she gave a gasping laugh, which turned to a look of dismay as he slid a

147

jewel-case from his pocket and opened it, displaying a diamond flower-brooch, with leaves of small emeralds. It had the charming frailty of a real flower, the lovely stones mounted tremblant on a concealed spring, quivering as his fingers touched it.

'Just here, I think.' He bent over her and pinned the brooch above her left bosom, where her heart beat so madly. 'Pretty, isn't it? It sets off your dress.'

'It didn't cost a pound,' she gasped. 'Oh, Luque, it must have cost a lot more than that.'

'My dear, a real woman doesn't count the cost,' he drawled. 'Don't you like it? If not I can always give it to one of those women in my vast collection.'

'It's beautiful, but I just don't expect you to be so extravagant—I mean, I wouldn't know the difference between real stones and paste ones, and I'd be quite happy with—with something less expensive.'

'Really?' His face had hardened and his lips had an edge to them. 'If you imagine I'd be seen with a wife in paste jewellery, then you're even more naïve than you look, and sound. For the love of heaven, Toni, you are no longer a charity case in a convent, and the angels won't throw down bolts of fire because I give you a bauble. Wear it in health, and a sense of fun, or I shall get annoyed. I'm not a very nice person when I'm annoyed, believe me.'

'I believe you,' she said, and wished that it hadn't been drummed into her that self-denial was a virtue, and a love of worldly things a sin. 'Thank you for the brooch. It's the prettiest thing I've ever seen.'

'Yes,' he said drily, his eyes intent upon her face. 'And don't you forget that it gives me pleasure—if you care about that—to give you the proper kind of clothes and jewels. I told you, you are mine—a gift of the saints to the devil.'

She knew from the tone of his voice that he was

being ironical, just to tease her, but a certain truth haunted his words. Friday had not yet come ... she couldn't yet know why he wanted her.

'Come, let us go and have our dinner. I, for one, am ravenous. It's the Cornish air, which blows off the sea and the moors and is filled with a sorcery all of its own.' He took her by the elbow she hadn't hurt and led her from the Chinese Room, across the hall and in through the open doors of the dining-room. So after all she was going to have to learn without delay the formal routines of life in a manor house.

She tensed as they entered the room, which had an air of being handsome but intimidating. The gleaming table was lit by silver candelabra, and the plates and glasses stood upon circlets of ivory-coloured lace.

'This is an interesting room,' said Luque, holding one of the tall chairs so she could slip into it. 'The walls are panelled in wreckwood from a ship broken on the rocks long ago, which had been carrying sandalwood and cedar from a faraway island. The table and chairs are made from a hanging oak-tree, and the silver the booty of the Cornish captain who sailed with Drake's navy.'

Luque sat down at the other end of the table and his smile was that of a man who had booty in the shape of a girl. He sat there in his black and white, telling her the history of the house as they ate the delicious meal which Lanyon served to them. A savoury asparagus dish, and then chicken perfectly cooked in a rich sauce, with braised onions, poached mushrooms, sugar peas and small potatoes.

Toni ate the heavenly food and noticed that the foreign intonations were more distinct in Luque's voice when he talked of the past ... as if for a while he left off being Lord Helburn and became again the young man of eighteen, walking into this house for the first time and seeing all the things his mother had cared for; feeling the witchery in the very air of Mawgan Plas.

How very different it must have seemed to him after his home in southern Spain, where the sun was so hot, the houses almost Arabic, and the laws governing marriage as strict as they had been in Victorian England.

Having not been told of his mother's illness, by the time he came to Cornwall she was laid to rest and he had only a box of letters (which she had never posted to him) to bring him the realisation of how she had suffered in order to find a stolen happiness with her Cornish artist.

After dinner, and the delectable apricot sweet, Luque took Toni into a charming music-room—but cold, silent because unused for so long—and showed her a pair of portraits of his mother. One was of a golden girl with eager eyes, clad in a delicate violet-coloured dress, a circlet of diamonds in her hair. The other was of a more mature woman, lovely in amber velvet to match her eyes ... eyes which held a certain sadness even as she smiled from the picture frame.

'She was very beautiful.' Toni spoke almost with reverence, for her young heart couldn't help but respond to the woman who had borne Luque. 'But I can understand your bitterness, *señor*, if you were taught to believe bad things about her. She probably never forgave herself for leaving you.'

'She did the only thing possible,' he replied. 'Children grow up and find their own strength, but a sour marriage never grows any sweeter, and as things turned out she wasn't fated to grow old and lose all that beauty. Let us say that my feelings are now bitter-sweet. I can never forget the loneliness of being without her, but I no longer blame her that I grew up—

rather like you, Tonita. I was deprived of the love that a child craves and the adolescent needs. We have that in common, *chica*.'

He turned from the portraits to study Toni. 'You had the rigid guidance of the nuns, and I had the harsh authority of a father who never let a day go by without a reference to my unchaste mother, as he called her. That adulteress who in the days of Babylon would have been stoned in the market square.'

His hand gripped Toni's shoulder and she winced, for he seemed not to realise that he was hurting her bruised arm. Then abruptly he crossed the room to a gleaming piano that stood within a rose-curtained alcove between the long windows. He turned the little key that unlocked the lovely instrument and lifted back the lid.

Toni watched in surprise as he sat down on the stool and ran his strong fingers along the keys, producing harmony instead of discord.

'My single consolation as a youth was that I had a German tutor who knew and understood music. He taught me to play the piano, and I was always smitten with the *Weisse Taube*, a piece which he composed himself. In English the words mean White Dove.'

Luque played for her, here in the room of the portraits, with the long curtain closing out the restless sea and the rolling moors, and the sky that would be deep purple as nightshade berries.

Toni listened to the strange beauty of the music, and watched the dark, withdrawn face of the man she loved, and she knew that for him the White Dove had represented his mother, flying far away across the sea and leaving him to grow up unloved.

It was then that Toni knew she could never leave him ... with or without his love she was his to make happy or sad.

'Lovely, isn't it?' he murmured.

And a little later in the Chinese Room, where they had coffee, he said with a faint touch of moodiness: 'At precisely this time next week, Tonita, you and I will be in Paris ... man and wife.'

It could have been the rich food and wine, or the sweet melancholy of the music, but Toni found it difficult to fall asleep in the big fourposter bed in the sea-tower.

She lay there in the darkness and heard the surf down on the sands of the cove, washing in over the sharp angles of the rocks, then running out again to meet the sea. It was a sound as regular as her own heartbeats, and in a while it must have lulled her off to sleep. But hers was not a restful slumber, for she began to toss about, dragging the bedcovers with her so that the eiderdown fell with a silky rustle to the floor.

A dream began and there was no escape for Toni ... she was shut in one of the prayer cells at the convent, but she wasn't alone there. A shadowy figure lurked in a corner, cowled from head to foot. The figure stood there silently, and Toni was aware of a coldness that struck her to the bone, and as she crouched there on the hard bench, her heart felt as if it were beating in her very ears.

All at once the figure stirred and began to approach her, and as it did so a hand with broken finger-bones threw back the cowl and Toni was staring with terror into a pair of empty eye-sockets ... she screamed, for this was the nun who had been bricked into the wall long, long ago. The nun who had dared to love a man ... again she screamed as the arms reached out and caught hold of her ....

'Toni, child, wake up!'

She awoke and the terror was still in her eyes as they found the face of Luque bent to her, lamp shadows in the lean angles of temple and jaw, a robe thrown hastily around him so that his bare chest was against her as he held her.

'I knew you'd have a nightmare in this damned tower,' he said roughly. 'It's an echo chamber for the sea down there——'

'I—I wasn't dreaming of the sea.' Toni shuddered and clung to him. 'It was the nun—she had no eyes and the bones of her fingers were all broken——'

'Hush, *chica*. It's over and I'm with you.'

'Don't leave me,' she pleaded. 'Oh, Luque, I couldn't bear it if I saw her again!'

His brows drew together as he looked down into her frightened eyes. Her face was without a trace of colour, and she was trembling in his arms.

'*Santa Maria*, that an imaginative young thing like you should have to grow up in that place! Be at peace, *mia*. I am just picking up the eiderdown and tucking in the covers——'

'Stay, Luque—please!'

'I have no intention of leaving you.' The robe was flung from him and he slid into the bed beside her, his silk-trousered legs hard against her own as he drew her to him. The fright diminished, and all sense of right or wrong. Toni knew only that he was with her, holding her and protecting her from the dark, haunted night. She slid her arms about his neck and with an inarticulate murmur he drew her to his heart.

'Sleep,' he murmured. 'Now you are safe, *chica*.'

But did she want to be safe? Her lashes fluttered against the skin of his shoulder. 'I'm not a child, Luque,' she wanted to say, whispering the words

153

against his warm throat. 'Don't treat me like one.'

But the memory of his earlier rejection was still painful, and right now she had no wish to spoil this heavenly closeness. She snuggled to him and let the sensual drowsiness sweep over her.

'Feeling more at ease?' he asked her softly, his voice like dark velvet in the velvety darkness.

'Oh yes—are you comfortable, *señor*?'

'Go to sleep,' he replied, in a dry tone of voice that made the velvet tone prickly. 'I'll pretend you're the woolly lamb I used to cuddle in bed all those years ago. The one they took away from me!'

He didn't have to explain that the toy lamb had vanished from his life along with his mother, and Toni didn't mind at all if he made a substitute of her. She sighed drowsily and fell dreamlessly asleep in the warm, strong arms.

And she awoke in the morning quite alone, the pillow smoothed out beside her and the covers carefully arranged so that Tamsin would be unaware, when she brought a cup of tea to Toni, that her bed had been shared by the master of the house.

It was as Tamsin was turning away from the bed that her gaze fell upon a dark leather object that lay upon the pale carpet. She bent to pick it up, and silently showed it to Toni. It was Luque's cheroot case and it must have dropped out of his robe pocket, last night.

'Shall I return this to his lordship, miss?' Tamsin's voice was as expressionless as her eyes.

Toni flushed. 'If you please, Tamsin.'

She watched, her toes curled together, as the dark clad woman departed from the room and closed the door behind her with a sharp little click.

Oh well, thought Toni, sipping her tea, it was naughty but nice to be looked upon as Luque's mistress, even if she had slept with him in the purest sense of the word.

It was her own secret ... her own torment that he had not made love to her.

CHAPTER TEN

THE trees crowded green along the banks of the Seine, and a lovely blue mist seemed to drift above the water, curling into soft, mysterious shapes. A mood *triste*, for this was Paris as the blue hour approached.

Toni stood on the balcony of the Hotel Torquilstone, owned by a Scotsman who had settled in Paris and made a paying game of his small and exclusive hotel. She was glad that it wasn't raining in Paris, as it had been raining that morning in Cornwall.

There had been not a ray of sunshine to light them from the Church of the Lilies, and only a few hardy souls had waited beneath their dripping umbrellas to watch the bride and groom make a dash for their car. A photographer had snapped them as they ran, the chiffon of Toni's skirts wet with rain beneath the white fur coat which Luque had flung around her. She had turned a startled face to the camera, and as she thought of that moment a smile quirked her lips. It would be a funny wedding photograph; not at all the usual gracious pose of a lord and his very new lady.

She leaned on the balcony rail and saw the evening lights coming to life along the riverside. How knowing of Luque to choose a hotel such as this one, where at first they wouldn't be likely to run into many of his smart friends. It also had an atmosphere that she liked, being comfortable without being too unglamorous. How strange it felt to be Lady Helburn, on her honeymoon, and still feeling a breathless sense of unreality.

Then, her every nerve attuned to Luque's return to their suite, she turned as she heard the door of the sitting-room open and close. He had been downstairs to have a chat to Torquil Sanderson, the man who owned the hotel and was an old friend of Luque's, and now he came to her with his supple stride and his quizzical smile.

'Have you now got your bearings after your first flight?' he asked her, tilting her chin so he could study her face.

She nodded and gave a little shiver as he turned her left hand and brushed his lips across her wrist. 'How very new your ring looks,' he said. 'I'm glad we had Tamsin and Lanyon as our witnesses, but why on earth did she add red roses to your bouquet? After all, you chose to have lilies of the valley on their own and you should have thrown out the roses. You mustn't allow Tamsin to intimidate you.'

'Oh, I didn't think it was worth making a fuss over. I suppose she doesn't think me worthy of Virgin's Flower.'

'And why not, pray?' He frowned down at Toni, a tall, distinctive figure in his bark-brown suit of very fine stripes, worn with a lighter brown silk shirt and impeccable cream tie.

'She knew we spent my first night at Mawgan Plas together, and who would believe, *señor*, that we——' Toni flushed slightly and turned to look again at the darkening Seine. 'This part of Paris is very attractive —will you show me around tomorrow? I want to see everything and fill every moment.'

Every moment, she thought, so I shan't have time to remember that Luque doesn't love me the way a man should love the girl he marries.

'If you aren't feeling tired, *chica*, we'll start our sightseeing tonight. I've never been to Paris with someone like you—a pure white page waiting to be written upon. You will see the city with new eyes, and I may recapture a little of my first wonderment. A lot has been changed, even here in Paris, but there is still enough of the old magic left to be enjoyed.'

'I've made up my mind that I'm going to enjoy this place, *señor*.'

'Why do you cling to the old formality?' he asked. 'I'm your husband now, for better or worse.'

'I know, but you look so much the *señor*, with your black hair and the way you wear your clothes. If you don't like being reminded that you're half Spanish, then I'll drop the Latin style of address.'

'I don't really mind what you call me, Tonita, if it makes you happy.' He studied her left hand, which seemed very slim and young to be weighted down by his rings. 'I mean you to be happy, child. You believe that, don't you?'

'Yes, Luque.' *Love me*, her heart silently cried, and I'll want for nothing else. Let me be your wife, not just your ward!

'Where are we going tonight?' she asked brightly.

'To a supper club I know of where the music and dancing are good, the wine excellent, and the *crêpes suzettes* just what the wizard ordered for pensive young brides.'

'I—I'm not pensive,' she denied. 'You must give me time to get used to the strangeness of everything—of being your wife. I can't yet take it in—it's as though I dreamed the church this morning and the ritual of it all.'

'A pity about the rain.' He leaned his back against the balcony rail and at once his face was in shadow and Toni couldn't make out the expression in his eyes. 'It would have made things better for you if the sun had deigned to shine on your finery. Did I tell you that

158

you looked very charming, despite those roses like drops of blood against your gown. Damn Tamsin!'

'Don't say that, Luque. You can't expect a woman with a broken heart to feel any joy in the marriage of other people.'

'She was offering you a subtle insult. There is a tradition in Latin countries that coloured flowers are given to loose women, the pale ones being reserved for the chaste. I don't want it all over again—first my mother, and now my wife!'

'Will it matter, *señor*? We shan't be living at Mawgan Plas all that much——'

'On the contrary, I may decide to settle down for a change, and I'd prefer to do it in Cornwall. My manager in Spain is a wise and clever fellow and I can trust him to run things well.'

'Do you mean it, Luque?' Toni tried to read his face, but the dusk had deepened and all she could make out was the odd gleam of his eyes in the lean mask of his face. 'Oh, it would be marvellous to have a *real* home, and I wasn't sure of what you were going to do. I thought you meant to leave me there alone——'

'Leave my bride?' he mocked her. 'What an unnatural *hombre* I'd be to do that, and think of the gossip! He's left her already, the wiseacres would say. Isn't that just like the devil!'

'You aren't a devil—not in my eyes.'

'Hooray for wifely loyalty,' he laughed. 'You're learning fast, Tonita. The best of wives is tolerant of her husband's wild and wilful ways. She doesn't try to change him and thereby earns his heartfelt gratitude. Nothing is more tedious than for a man to take unto himself a charming spouse only to find out that she's a salvationist and out to save his soul. Mine was dropped into a pool of iniquity long ago and you'd

159

drown, *chica,* if you wanted to go fishing for it.'

'I wouldn't want a second ducking, the first was alarming enough.' She spoke lightly and didn't attempt to protest that if he was a sinner, then she preferred him to the saints. He had none of their harshness and their inability to accept normal human weakness. Nor their humourless certainty that the itchy shirt and the scrubbing brush were good for subduing the normal hopes and desires of charity girls.

'Come inside.' Luque caught hold of her very suddenly and lifted her into his arms. 'When we arrived I forgot to lift you over the threshold of our first place together as man and bride, and I suspect that you are superstitious, my Irish witch. It's supposed to bring luck, isn't it, for the groom to do this?' He stepped over the threshold of the balcony into the sitting-room, but because it was dark he blundered into an armchair that stood near the french doors and stumbled with her, falling like a judo expert and managing not to knock all the breath out of Toni as they sprawled on the deep carpet.

They lay there, his hard body pressing against hers, and suddenly they both began to laugh.

'So much for superstition, *mia.* It looks as if we were meant for a fall—are you all right? You're so little——'

'I—I'm only winded——'

'Such a slim young thing,' his hand stroked across her brow and down her face to her throat. 'Never grow up, Tonita. Never discard altogether the chrysalis of the funny, cropped, winged thing that I took on my yacht.'

'I'll try, Luque, but nature has a way of catching up with all of us and I can't always be a comic adolescent who amuses you. Will you put me away from you when I turn from a bumpkin into a person?'

'Ah, don't grow up too soon! I never had a playmate when I was a *chico*; my father was held in too much fear and awe for his son to be very popular. In place of good fellowship I had good-time girls. Do you comprehend?'

'Yes——' Both revelations were painful to accept. 'Poor Luque!'

'Poor rich boy!'

'I'll be whatever you ask of me.'

'Will you? D'you remember on the *Miranda* when you told me fiercely that you'd never be kicked around by me? That if I tried it on, you'd kick back?'

'So I would, *señor*. Whatever you give, I'll give back. That's only fair.'

'Kicks or kisses, eh?'

'Yes——' She spoke with a sudden faintness, for his face had come near to her and she felt his breath across her eyelids. She felt a languor and a longing to be loved, and also a panic that gave her the will and the strength to push away out of his arms. No! If he kissed her, she would be unable to hold back her response to a caress he only gave casually. She scrambled to her feet and instinct guided her to the light switches. The wall-lights sprang into brightness and that dangerous moment was averted. There was too much heaven, and too much hell in being so close to Luque. She could bear it better if she kept some distance between them.

'If we're going out, Luque, then we'd better get ready.'

'Eager for the crowds, are you?' He was on his feet in a single bound and brushing casually at the knees of his trousers. 'Off with you, then. Go and make yourself lovely.'

'That would take a miracle.' She brushed a despondent hand across her hair, which was still very short

161

and like the curly pelt of a poodle. 'I wish I had a glamorous blonde wig to hide this mop of red feathers.'

'It wouldn't become you to be blonde,' he said. 'Stop wishing you looked like Birdina and dozens like her. You have your very own style and so long as it pleases me, you have no say in the matter.'

'That is typical male arrogance,' she retorted.

'Calling your husband a chauvinist?'

'If you like. My hair, my face, and my body are my own. Just because you've put a ring on my hand—it isn't through my nose so you can lead me about like a bit of livestock.'

'It conjures up quite an image of fun.' His eyes flicked her up and down. 'Wear the jade dress for our evening out.'

'My wedding dress? It got wet with the rain.'

'It will have dried out by now, and a drop of rain never hurt real silk. The dress suits you and you only wore it for the ceremony, which was over all too soon. I'm requesting, *mia*, not giving you a chauvinistic order.'

'That's different.' She tilted her chin at him, but her lashes quivered as her eyes dwelt on his. It might amuse him to spar with her, but she knew his authority and his temper. If she had refused to wear the dress, he would have forced her into it and because it was her wedding dress the fragrance of those moments in church clung to the silky garment.

She went into her bedroom and closed the door behind her. Their suite was one of the hotel's largest, consisting of the sitting-room, the bathroom, and the adjoining bedrooms. Here in a room papered with apricot roses, and furnished all in white with gilt finish, her suitcases had been unpacked and her nightwear laid out on the apricot bedcover.

Toni picked up the filmy nightdress and her cheeks

burned as she studied her fingers through the diaphanous material. She and Luque would drink champagne at the supper club, and then it would be their wedding night ... which she would spend alone in this room, clad in the seductive nightdress which might as well be of flannel, buttoned to the neck and revealing only her face and her feet.

She went to the louvre-doored wardrobe and took out the jade chiffon silk. Luque's wedding gift, the snow-white fur coat, had saved most of the dress from the downpour, and it was only the bottom of the skirt which had got so wet as they had run along the church path, her hand held so tightly in his that her rings had felt as if they were cutting into her finger-bones.

To her delight the skirt was undamaged and the soft folds had fallen back into shape. She stroked the dress and the moments ticked by as she recalled the marriage service, the few scattered onlookers in the church, the solemnity of the Bach organ music, and the creamy lilies scenting the air. All through the ceremony the rain had pounded on the Gothic windows and blurred the stained-glass angels and martyrs. Toni had felt cold, and only the clasp of Luque's fingers had been warm as he had placed the gold ring upon her finger.

With this ring I thee wed. With my body I thee worship ... Toni shivered at the memory of the words, which Luque had spoken in such a firm, sure voice. Her own voice had quivered, and there beyond the white-cassocked shoulder of the priest had stood the image of Our Lady, sweeping back over her a wave of convent memories. Had she not dared to run away, she would have been made a novice in the service of Our Lady and confined for ever among the other nuns. No tall, dark man would have stood at her side and heard her make vows to love him until they both should die.

'For always,' she murmured to herself. 'It's for ever and ever, but does he realise that?'

She thought of what Birdina had said to her, implying that when he no longer found Toni an amusement to tease and dress, he would take a mistress.

They were in Paris, where the *mariage de convenance* had its roots, and Toni was going to have to face up to being a wife by day and a spinster by night. Only the ring itself had any significance for Luque; he would look after her, but he saw nothing to worship in her boyish body, her red hair, her eyes that had seen so little of life and pleasure.

When she had put on the jade dress she stared at herself in the mirror and her own delicate strangeness in the chiffon silk did nothing to boost her morale. How fearfully young she looked! About as much like a bride as a girl at her confirmation. Big defiant eyes —lips unpainted—ah, but they didn't have to stay that way, for when Justine St. Cyr had sent down the trousseau to Mawgan Plas, they had included a small case of cosmetics, at which until now Toni had only glanced.

When she entered the sitting-room, the white fur coat draped around her shoulders, Luque was out on the dark balcony and she could smell cheroot smoke. She stood there as casually as possible, but inwardly she was nervously tensed for his reaction when he strolled in from the darkness and saw her under the lights.

His eyes narrowed as he took her in. He took a pull at his cheroot and smoke drifted from his lips, beside which the lines of indulgent amusement slowly deepened. 'If you had to use stuff on your face, then I'm thankful you haven't applied it with a trowel.'

'Do you like it?' she asked. 'I—I wanted to look—

glamorous.'

'My dear,' he strolled right to her and stood looking down into her eyes, to the lids of which she had added a shading of the pale green shadow she had found in the cosmetic case. Her skin had been powdered to a pearly sheen, and her lips were discreetly red, 'you have certainly left the little *golfo* a memory and a shade on the sunken deck of the *Miranda*. I confess to a stab of regret, for I was rather fond of that odd young creature in the chopped-off jeans and jersey.'

'I can't go around like that any more, *señor*. You said so yourself, and I hoped you'd like my new look.'

'I like it,' he said dryly. 'You've turned from a quaint waif into someone so astonishingly pretty that I shouldn't take you out into a city filled with amorous Frenchmen.'

'Do you mean you aren't taunting me?' Her eyes widened and were as limpidly green as her dress. 'You really to think that I look nice?'

'Nice is a lukewarm word, *mia*.' He reached out a hand and his fingertips traced the bones of her face and the delicate line of her jaw, down to her soft earlobe. Tiny thrills of pleasure rippled up and down her spine at his touch, but she stood very still and pretended she was a statue.

'I'm your Galatea,' she said. 'You changed me from awkward clay into a woman.'

'Correction, Tonita! You were never an insensitive lump of clay, and I look at you now and curiosity stirs in me regarding your parents. Nothing was known about them at the convent?'

She shook her head. 'I was treated as a foundling from the moment they took me from the *torno*, and in all the time I was there no one from the outside ever came to see me, or make claim to me. One of the Sisters was sure that I was illegitimate—we were always treated a little differently from the other girls, except the one or two whose fathers were paying for their keep.'

'Poor little Toni!' He drew the fur coat around her and held the soft collar up around her face. 'You are well claimed now, *chica*, and never again will you be treated as less than nothing. You belong to me!'

He said it with a ring of arrogance in his voice. 'Shall we go, Tonita? The night and the music awaits us.'

They walked together to the lift and Toni could feel the nervous quiver in her legs. She had never been to a night club and it seemed the essence of sophistication to her, and it so pleased her that Luque liked the look of her. The lift was travelling downwards when he took her wrist in his fingers and snapped a chain around it. She gave it a wild look and saw the dense green stones glimmering among the sparkling ones.

'Luque!'

'That's my name.' He lounged lazily against the wall of the lift as it came to a halt.

'You keep on doing this—you keep giving me things, and I—what do I give you?'

'You'd be surprised,' he drawled. 'Now don't make a fuss, or the folk in the foyer will think we're having a tiff and it will get into the newspapers.'

'You've already given me a ring and a brooch——'

'Just for starters. You're my lady now, and other women will be watching you like cats who've seen a pigeon fly into their yard.'

'Then it's for appearances' sake that you like me to wear the jewellery?'

'If it will put your funny mind at rest to think so.' They made their way through the foyer of the hotel where people stood about chatting, or smoking while they waited for someone. But a sudden hush fell as the lean, tall figure of Lord Helburn and his bride made for the swing doors that led out to where a uniformed porter was flagging taxi-cabs for those who were dining out or going to the theatre. No one spoke to Luque, for there were times when he could assume an air of total indifference to friend or foe, and the avid head-to-heel glances that were being directed at Toni were, she knew, enough to spark him to sarcasm or sheer insolence had anyone tried to interrupt their progress from the hotel.

Outside the night air fanned against Toni's hot cheeks and she was glad to be out of range of the curious eyes.

A taxi slid into the kerb and they entered the leathery dimness, the door clicking tightly shut behind Luque. 'That,' she breathed, 'was like walking through fire.'

'In time it won't be quite so scorching, but that's what you get, *mia*, when you marry a scandalous man. Any fool can see that you're half my age, and they were also trying to see just how depraved the son of Don Beltran and "that woman" has made you. Do you feel very depraved?'

'You know how I feel.' Her fingers crept into his. 'No one knows you as I do.'

'Rot!' He gave a sardonic laugh. 'The truth is that I'm a selfish son-of-a-devil who should have put you in a good girls' school and then found you a nice boy to marry.'

'What a bore that would be,' she scoffed, 'to be married to a tame boy. It wouldn't suit me!'

'It would be much better for you,' he said, a trifle sternly. 'I have had toys before you came along, and I've broken them. Who can tell at this stage what I shall do with you—I have the devil's own temper at times, being the son and heir of that cruel swine who had his own box at the bullfights and who sold his own horses into the rings after he had shattered their strength and pride. He tried to do the same with me, except that he forgot *I was his son*. He got what he gave as soon as I reached his height and his level of— oh, to hell with him!' He swung an arm about Toni and pressed her shoulders. 'Let's not think about the future, let's just enjoy ourselves. We're on our honeymoon, after all, and that's what the things were made for.'

'Yes, Luque.' She leaned her head against him and suppressed a sigh. Honeymoons were also made for loving, but he seemed to have set a limit on how far he would go in his game of marriage. He seemed to have it deeply ingrained on his soul that he would make hell instead of heaven for the woman he let into his heart, and Toni had to be content with what she had.

'Thank you for the bracelet, *señor*.'

'It's a jewelled slave chain,' he drawled, lifting her wrist and brushing his lips where the chain rested. 'That's what you are, are you not?'

'If you say so, Luque.' Her skin tingled from the touch of his lips, and she didn't care that she was enslaved by him. All her life she had belonged to no one ... now if she was possessed by a devil, he was at least a strangely gallant one who was never a harsh taskmaster. He took her for better or worse, just as she took him; for all he knew her mother could have been one of those creatures who sold herself for money, and her father a sailor off a ship ... some casual lover of a Magdalen.

She glanced up at Luque in the passing lights of the boulevard that flickered in and out of the cab, and he seemed to be withdrawn into dark thoughts of the

168

past. When all at once his eyes flashed down to meet Toni's, they seemed to blaze with a tortured regret.

Oh no! Her heart gave a painful throb. Did he regret already that he had landed himself with an innocent bride he dared not treat as a wife!

'You look like one of those messengers in a Gothic window,' he said quietly, 'bringing a cup of wine to one of the half-gods. D'you think, Toni, that the half-gods will ever be gone from the temple to let the real gods in?'

'Does it matter, *señor*, one way or the other?'

'I rather think it does, *chica*. Ah, here we are Chez Elle.' The cab drew to a halt and he leaned over her to release the catch of the door. 'Come, let us go and drink the wine!' he said, laughing.

CHAPTER ELEVEN

THE orchestra was playing as they entered ·the restaurant of the club; it was one of those lighthearted compositions from a decade past and gone, and unrecognized by Toni who knew so little of the world, let alone this glamorous side of it.

They were led by a waiter to a secluded table, on which were white carnations and a rose-crystal lamp. Toni sat down and looked around her with eager interest; she knew that several people were staring at Luque and herself, but the soft rose lighting of the restaurant seemed to soften the effect of their curiosity. Luque had said that she would get used to it; that at first they would occasion the stares and the muttered comments. But oh, how she longed to stand on the very table and shout to the world that she loved Luque and didn't care what his life had been before she came along. She knew that his sardonic armour was worn to keep himself safe from the deep hurts he had suffered as a boy, and with this knowledge shining· in her eyes she dared the glances of the women, and the speculative stares of the men.

Her chin was tilted and the rose light mingled with her red hair and played its blush over her white skin. The jade chiffon silk was beautifully styled and she wore the gemmed jewellery which Luque had given her ... the pigeon who had flown into the vicinity of the rich cats, and a quick glance at Luque showed Toni that he was amused by the situation.

He lounged back in his seat as the waiter drew the gold-foiled bottle from the ice-bucket so that it hissed. His brow quirked at the sound, as if for him it expressed what people were thinking as they looked at him with his youthful bride.

The champagne was poured into long-stemmed bowls, pale gold and shimmering with tiny bubbles. Luque raised his glass and Toni picked hers up. 'To you, my lady fair,' he said, and his eyes dwelt on her in the caressive lamplight as he put his lips to his glass.

'To you, my lord.' She grinned at him, and sipped the delicious wine, which seemed to run through her veins like a soft fire. 'I like that music the band is playing—you do realise, *señor*, that I know more religious music than any other sort.'

'Don't remind me,' he groaned, 'of what a little Goody-Two-Shoes I've married.'

'I'm not one of those,' she protested. 'Birdina didn't think so—she said I'd be infuriating if I was.'

'Infuriating isn't quite the word I'd use.' He looked into his wine glass, and then up again with a glimmer of devilry in his eyes. 'It's traditional for a newly wed couple to dance on their wedding day, so how about it?'

'I can't dance,' Toni gasped. 'You don't imagine that they give dancing lessons at a convent.'

'Dancing is something that comes quite naturally—all you do is give yourself to the rhythm of the music, and to me. I'll guide you.' He rose with these words and came round to where she sat. His hands drew her firmly to her feet and he led her on to the dance floor where other couples were circling in each other's arms to the charming, lilting music from an old-time movie. Toni felt herself drawn into Luque's arms, held close and guided into the movements of the dance. At first she stumbled over his feet, but he didn't lose patience with her and in a while she felt herself relaxing and responding to this strange new pleasure.

'You dance awfully well, *señor*,' she murmured. 'I expect it's due to the Spanish blood in your veins.'

'More likely it's due to all the practice I've had,' he responded drily. 'You're very light on your feet, Tonita ... that's it, follow me without thinking about it ... attractive tune this, an Irving Berlin number from the Thirties. You've never even seen a film, have you *chica*? *Santa Maria*, when I think of everything to which you are a complete novice—a newborn babe almost, with so much to learn, and a devil your tutor.'

'I'd want no other tutor,' she assured him.

'So eager are you to learn all the tricks in my repertoire? Do you know what some of these people are thinking as they watch us—those that know me by reputation? That is the rake who ruins women, and the irony of it is that I've only to look at a woman and she thinks she's ruined. The devil blacked my eye that's what they say at San Luis Bara where I was born and where I grew up, and it's been amusing to play along with the idea. A man can only ruin what is innocent, and I was never in that select company—until now.'

Toni gave him a quick look, and then her heart gave a twist inside her when she caught him staring beyond her to an alcove where a woman of startling fairness had appeared. She stood there alone until the music died away and the couples began to return to their tables.

Who was she? Toni sat down and watched as the woman mounted the steps to the platform where the orchestra was grouped. Silence had fallen over the restaurant, then all at once a wave of applause swept the place, and Toni's nerves gave a jump as Luque joined n the applause.

The woman stood there on the platform, looking round at people with an enigmatical smile on her ed mouth. She looked like the reincarnation of a oddess of love, dressed in close-cut luminous silk that uggested a body perfectly made and white as marble. Her hair was a glistening tower of gilt scrolls, in which ems sparkled. Her eyes slanted in her face and they eemed to hold an insolent awareness of the effect she reated as she strolled to the dark piano, and lounged here in all her golden beauty.

Toni looked across the table at Luque and those range eyes of his were fixed upon the goddess—for here seemed no other word to describe her—and morseless and sudden came the truth, like a slap cross Toni's face.

Luque had known this woman—Luque had loved er!

'Who is she?' Toni asked, and the words came husky, from a hurting throat.

'Melisande,' he replied. 'Not her real name, of urse, but who cares about that? She sings for her pper, and her diamonds and sapphires. Always sapphires because they match her eyes. Superb, is she not? ather like a moon goddess.'

'She looks as if she isn't wearing a stitch underneath at dress,' said Toni, hating herself for saying such a ing, and yet so certain that the woman was a onene flame of Luque's that she hated him as well. alousy had struck, and Toni didn't like the feeling.

'You're probably right,' Luque drawled. 'Melly ways did say that lingerie spoilt the line of a closeting dress, and it would be a crime against artistic hievement for her lines to be blurred.'

'If that's your attitude towards dress, then I wonder u wasted money on those silky things you bought for me—may I have more champagne, please?'

She held out her glass but he ignored it, his eyes mocking her across the table. 'When the caviare arrives, otherwise you'll be intoxicated. And let me point out that you aren't exactly a Melisande, and being half a Spaniard I'd never allow my wife to go around in a half-nude state—not outside the home, that is.'

'You mean I haven't her kind of shape?'

'That is stating the obvious, *mi esposa*.'

'It doesn't really feel as if I'm your wife.'

'We have a very legal document to prove it, with both our names on it and our antecedents'.'

'It must have been awkward for you, *señor*, not being able to produce my pedigree. Did you explain that I was merely a piece of flotsam which you found on your travels?'

'Something of the sort,' he said unkindly. The waiter came with their caviare, which was served from a small silver pot, with thin slices of smoked salmon and lemon, with brown bread toast, served hot in a snowy napkin. At the same time a hush descended over the dining-room as the keys of the dark piano broke into a trickle of melody, and the lights sank down to a single circlet of brightness on the golden figure of Melisande, revealing the half-closed eyes, the parted lips, the jewelled hand on a curved hip.

As she began to croon a French song in a seductive voice, Toni crunched a piece of toast and caviare and was very aware of the frown which Luque directed at her. Toni shrugged to herself ... the caviare looked funny, but it tasted all right, and she had learned in a hard school to accept the inevitable. Hadn't she been warned that Luque had not led the life of a monk? Anyway, it now became transparent why he had chosen to dine at Chez Elle tonight ... he had known that his golden flame Melisande would be singing here, and he had to find some way to make his honeymoon exciting.

At the finale of her song Melisande was applauded with so much enthusiasm that Toni could only guess that it was her sensual appeal rather than the quality of her voice which created so much idolatry. Now she moved to another section of the stage, where she arranged her spectacular figure against a marble pillar, and there she seemed to rest for a minute or so, caressing her audience with her slanting eyes. The music began to play and this time it had a strange, haunting quality that caught Toni's attention and allowed her to forget for a short while that her husband had known this woman, and seemed to have a lingering affection for her.

Toni bit her lip ... affection was too mild a word. For Melisande a man would feel a hungry passion and a worship of her superb body. If he had ever made love to her, he would be unlikely to forget her.

It was this knowledge that made the ballad sung by the siren all that more significant for Toni, though she couldn't be sure that it was directed at Luque, she could only guess. Not once had Melisande glanced in the direction of their table, but the whispers would have reached her. She would have known that Lord Helburn was dining here ... with his bride ... a mere girl.

The lights came up, the applause thundered, and the vision in silk vanished from the stage.

Toni looked quickly at Luque, but instead of gazing bleakly at the stage like a man bereft he was calmly eating his smoked salmon.

'What was the song that she sang?' Toni asked him. 'It seemed a bit on the sad side, but I thought it suited her voice.'

'It was Desirée Dihau's *Columbin*. She always sings

it well, with that husky awareness in her voice of love's irony.'

'I couldn't imagine Melisande ever being a victim of love. She's the kind of woman that men adore.'

'True, Tonita. It's in the human soul to pay homage to beauty.'

'What about the heart, *señor*?' Toni felt driven to impale herself on the full sharpness of what he felt for that woman who seemed to fulfil all of a man's dreams. Her hair was so wonderfully blonde, the symmetry of her features a wonder in themselves, and she surely had a body like Venus, only with white arms that would hold a man warmly and possessively.

'The heart is a mystery, *chica*. It always has been so, and while men and women continue to walk this earth, so will it remain the suspense drama of the ages, about which most songs are sung, most tears are wept, most joys are felt.'

'Now you really speak like a man who has loved,' said Toni, her fingers clenching about the stem of her champagne glass. 'Or should I say a man in love?'

He made no answer, and this could have been because the waiter was at their table arranging the plates and cutlery for their next course. Food with a delectable aroma was served from a trolley, and when the waiter had gone and they were alone again, Luque casually changed the trend of the conversation and Toni's wildest fears were realised.

Luque was in love, and he had no intention of discussing the way he felt with his wife!

The meal proceeded to a mound of raspberries banked by sliced peaches, with a delicious sauce poured into each sweet berry, thick cream being added.

They were halfway through their dessert when Toni felt a sudden tension in herself, and when she glanced up from her plate she saw that Luque had his eye fixed upon someone who had approached their table and stood just beyond Toni's shoulder.

Luque rose to his feet and Toni had never seen his eyes look so inscrutable and lidded, so their odd flickering was made almost sinister. 'How are you, Melly? It's been a long time, but you still look indestructible.'

'*Mon diable*,' drawled that seductive voice, 'you always had cruel and charming things to say to a woman. It has been five years, not fifty, and life is still a game which I very much enjoy.'

'I can see that, *ma chère*. On stage you still have the world at your feet.'

'I still have it off stage, *mon cher*.' And with these words Melisande walked into view of Toni, and now she was dressed in the fluid grace of sapphire-blue velvet and on a chain hung a large flawless sapphire, its resting place in the superb valley of her bosom. Her skin against the velvet was damask white, and her shining hair had been combed into supple curves about her long, slender neck. Her lips were painted a dark sensuous red and they were startling against her skin, showing the glint of her teeth as she studied Toni.

'I didn't quite believe the rumours, *mon cher*, but they are nonetheless true. She is a *bébé*, *un petit poussin*, *non*?'

Melisande laughed softly as she called Toni a pretty baby, and her eyes flicked to Luque and their blueness seemed to acquire a brazen look as she stared at him. 'So you marry the *jeune fille naïve* and confound all your critics, eh?'

'I always did enjoy confounding people,' he rejoined. 'We were married today, and as an old friend you must sit down with us and have a glass of champagne.'

'I shall be delighted, dear Luque. Champagne is still the only drink at weddings and wakes.'

He gave her an ironical bow, and then beckoned a

waiter to bring another chair. When she was seated she turned again to Toni and took a look at the fruit and cream on her plate. 'You would not be afraid of the cream at your age, eh? So very young that the woman in you has not yet begun to reveal herself. But as I have always said, it is a wise thing for a girl to marry a much older man, for there is so much he can teach her ... all those things he has learned in the school of life ... and love.'

Melisande's voice lingered on the word, and her red lips silently caressed it as she accepted from Luque a glass of champagne. Her long lashes curled down over her blue eyes as she looked at him and raised her glass.

'It really is something to drink to, *le mariage* of a man who has eluded the chains of matrimony so adeptly. Your young bride must have a secret fascination of her very own.'

' "Innocence hath privilege in her," ' he quoted. 'It' a rare commodity these days, wouldn't you agree?'

'*Mon ami*, when did you and I ever agree?' sh laughed softly, her lips at the brim of her wine glass. 'A man and a woman should be always on the knife edge of battle, and then life is exciting. But to b always in agreement is so tame, so boring. Does you bride always agree with you and regard you as *u brave homme*?'

'Heaven forbid! Toni knows me for what I am.'

'Does she really?' Melisande raised a perfectly shape eyebrow. 'And yet she married you—how very brav of her, or very young.'

'Doubtless a little of both,' he drawled. 'You wi have noticed that she has red hair, the invariable sig of impulsiveness and a spirited nature.'

'Yes, such fiery hair for a girl.' Melisande gazed the tendril of hair that lay on Toni's forehead, a tir flame licking at her skin. 'Do you wear it so shor

178

petite, because it is difficult to control?'

'My hair has always been kept short,' said Toni, who was confused by the astonishing beauty of this woman .. there was so much of it; almost too much. On stage she had looked far slenderer than she was in actuality, and Toni had to avert her eyes from the deep plunge at the neckline of the velvet dress. A man's woman, in every sense of the word!

'You don't say?' Melisande let her eyes rove curiously over Toni, taking in the demure styling of the jade dress, and letting her gaze rest on the girl's slight bosom where Luque's gemmed flower was pinned. 'Rumour has it that you were in a convent? How very droll that devil should marry a little saint. Do you hope to reform him?'

'I—I quite like him the way he is,' Toni rejoined.

'What a sweet thing to say,' Melisande laughed, bitter-sweetly. 'Do you hear that, *mon ami*, your girl-bride *likes* you! Are you losing your infamous touch, Luque? You used to be able to make women mad about you, but I do recall that once you had turned their heads and twisted their hearts, you usually became enamoured of the sea and went off on one of your cruises. So the *Miranda* is no more, *mon cher*? She has gone on the rocks with all your old loves?'

'Yes, Melly. But she is the one old love that I regret losing.'

'*Touchée.*' The lovely red mouth was distorted for a moment. 'I see that marriage has not made you less cruel.'

'*Ma bonne*, I am sure you can take a little of what you have given to others. Were you so kind when you made Rafael believe that I had abused his friendship by stealing his wife? You knew he was more vulnerable than I because he loved you. More honourable than I because he had good honest parents who were deeply hurt when he divorced you in Mexico, going against them and his faith. That fight we had was over you, and I had to break his arm or be killed by him, and I didn't fancy dying because of you, Melly.'

'You—you hate me?' she whispered, while Tom watched the scene and felt little pieces of puzzle fall into place. Both Luque and this ravishing woman seemed to have forgotten her presence at the table; they had been swept back into the past by old love and hates. She had been the wife of his friend. She was the woman who had involved him in a notorious divorce scandal ... Melisande the singer, whom he had applauded.

Toni reached blindly for her own wine glass and in her nervousness she knocked it flying and felt the champagne spill on the skirt of her dress. She began to dab at the wetness with her napkin, until Luque suddenly gripped her wrist in hard fingers.

'Go to the powder-room and see to it! That poor damn dress seems doomed to ruination—like the pair of us, for all I know!'

'Come!' Melisande had swept to her feet in a fragrant cloud of perfume. 'We shall go together, *petite*, and see to your dress.'

Toni didn't protest, for somehow she was too hurt by what Luque had said to be able to resist the company of Melisande, who instead of taking her to the powder-room, took her backstage to a cluttered dressing-room that was redolent of cosmetics and vases of flowers, no doubt the offerings of her male admirers.

'Little noodle, you are trembling,' said Melisande as she dabbed at the champagne stains with cotton wool dipped in water. 'Are you in fear that he will beat you because you spoil the dress?'

'No—he wouldn't beat a woman. He doesn't ha—

to,' Toni muttered, her teeth clenched against the pain of his words.

'You love that devil one hell of a lot, don't you?' Melisande reached for a chocolate in a heart-shaped box and her teeth bit into it as she looked directly into Toni's eyes, which were dark-jade in her distress.

'And he loves you one hell of a lot, doesn't he?'

Toni stared back at Melisande, who was delicately licking chocolate off her fingertips.

'*Mon dieu*, don't tell me that you don't know this? In Paris with Luque de Mayo, on your honeymoon and unaware that he looks at you as if you might vanish at any moment and fly out of his reach? I knew him well in the old days, but I never saw him look at anyone as he looks at you—a mere girl who looks as if she believes that the bees make honey without that nuptial flight of theirs. Maybe that is the attraction! Ah yes, it strikes me that a man who has enjoyed himself in an orchid house might well find a wayside flower much to his liking after the heady perfume of the exotics.'

Melisande gave that throaty laugh of hers and as she leaned against the cluttered dressing-table a rose fell apart in one of the vases and the petals fell to the floor.

'What hurts most, that he should scold you, or that you should believe that he and I were really lovers?'

'Were you?' Toni asked, in a voice that was almost inaudible.

'We could have been, if he hadn't played the Spaniard for once and put honour before pleasure. It was quite a prick to my vanity, for in those days I had youth and freshness and none of the need to embellish the lily. I played Desdemona and allowed my husband to find a cravat of Luque's in my bed. As simple as that, but Rafael had not read the play and he didn't know that in this instance Desdemona had played Iago as well.'

'How could you do such a thing to your husband?' Toni looked at Melisande with shocked eyes.

'Quite simply because he bored me. He agreed with everything I ever said, and not once in our four years together did he give me a bruise. He knelt to me when I wanted him to dominate me. He let me make a fool of him with a dozen men—but Luque was, on that point, a perfect Spaniard. He turned his back on me and so I stabbed him!'

Toni caught her breath, and at the sound Melisande gave a mocking laugh. 'Only figuratively speaking, *petite*. You will find no scars from me on that lean and vital body—I must say that the years are good to certain men. Luque is even more attractive now he has those lines in his face, and there is no mistaking the Latin blood in him. Such men keep hard-muscled and don't develop that slackness of frame that a woman sees in other men—and look who has him!'

The blue eyes swept Toni up and down. 'Ah, go to him, you child. Make him happy—if you can!'

Toni fled from the dressing-room, holding her chiffon silk skirts as she made for the restaurant dining-room. But halfway there she was caught and held by her husband, who had her white fur coat slung over his arm, and a dark look in his eyes.

'I shouldn't have let you go with her,' he said, with a touch of violence. 'I expect she's told you a pack of lies about me?'

Toni shook her head and gazed up wildly into his face. Melisande had said that he loved *her* ... had that been a lie ... a trick played on an innocent young fool who so craved for his love?

'She helped me to clean the dress, that's all.'

'Really?' His eyes flicked her white face. 'Let's leave

this place—I don't know what devil drove me to bring you here, for I knew she was singing here. Torquil told me so. Come, the porter has a cab waiting!'

They left Chez Elle, and speeding away in the cab Toni imagined Melisande in her untidy dressing-room, a few more roses falling apart as she ate her way through that heart-shaped box of chocolates.

'It wasn't such a bad evening,' Toni said after a while. 'At least I learned how to dance.'

'You also learned a few other things,' he said grimly, seated well away from her on the leather seat, leaving her a slim, white-clad figure in a corner. 'I hope you found them enlightening?'

'I did, Luque,' she said, and her heart was beating quickly beneath the fur coat. 'I'm glad you didn't betray your Spanish friend.'

'One of my few good deeds, *mia.*'

'I'm another of them, aren't I?'

'It would seem so.' He spoke with a touch of moodiness and then fell silent, not speaking again until the cab set them down at the hotel.

It was late and the foyer was now empty as they crossed to the lift. They rode up to the corridor on which their suite was situated and when he unlocked the door and switched on the lights, he gave her a brief look and told her to go to bed.

'Luque ...' She stood there hesitant, her lips working, wanting to say the words that just wouldn't came. This was their wedding night and she didn't want to sleep in a lonely bed.

'You must be whacked,' he said. 'Goodnight, Toni.'

'Goodnight ...' She left him and walked into her bedroom, for she had no way of knowing how a woman broke down the barriers that a man erected. If he loved her, he would surely want her, but no sign of that had showed in his eyes. They had been expressionless, veiled, as if she played no part in his thoughts.

She dropped her fur coat to a chair and walked across to the bed, where the filmy nightdress lay like a soft invitation. How could she let Luque know that she cared for him with all her heart and body? That she had a love to give that wasn't of the shallow, grasping kind that women like Melisande handed out like battle prizes to the men who fought over them!

Toni drew the soft, scented silk to her cheek and her eyes began to glow with the green fire of the gems in the slave chain which Luque had fastened about her wrist ... she wasn't going to be a wife in name only, not if there was a ray of hope that Melisande was right and Luque really cared for her but was holding his hand out of some gallant idea that she was too young and unworldly to be able to understand a man's passion.

She was young and naïve, but she knew what she wanted ... to belong to Luque in every sense of the word, so that every glance between them had meaning, and every touch, however slight, was a signal that they belonged to each other.

Oh yes, that was what Toni yearned for, and tonight she must find the courage to fight for it.

She regarded her weapons; a wisp of silk and lace, a pair of grey-green eyes, and a very slim and innocent body. The mirror didn't reveal the warm, wild beating of her heart, except at the base of her throat where a tiny pulse had a life of its own.

With trembling hands she removed the jade dress, christened as it had been first by the rain and then by the champagne. She took off the silk underthings and saw the glimmer of her skin as she drew the nightdress over her head and it slid down, caressing and diaphanous, about her slight curves. She brushed her hair until it was shining and flamy, and all the time that tiny pulse in her throat beat like a wild little wing of fear and hope.

She had no definite plan of action until she heard the water running hard in the bathroom and she knew that Luque was taking a shower.

Then like a shadow—albeit a trembling one—she slipped into his bedroom and ran silently across the carpet to his bed. She slid beneath the covers ... the lamp was aglow on the bedside table and she decided that it would take him more by surprise, perhaps weaken his resistance, if he discovered her in the darkness.

Toni clicked off the lamp, and lay there in the grip of love and trepidation.

What if Melisande had been playing a game with her? What if he became wildly angry and flung her from his bed?

Her heart throbbed as the bathroom door opened, and then closed behind him. He came silently across the room, paused as if surprised that the light was out, then took hold of the covers and came into the bed with that hard thrust of the silk-trousered legs, that warm, clean aroma of a brown-skinned torso.

'What the devil——!' His hand found her, sliding down the silk of her nightdress. 'Toni, what are you doing in my bed? Had a scare of some sort, such as a French bat flying in from the trees?'

'No——' The word hardly scraped past her lips.

'What is it—are you expecting a nightmare?'

'No, Luque.' She swallowed the nervous dryness from her throat and took the plunge. 'Preferably a honeymoon—a real one.'

Came a silence which spelled doom and failure if he were given half a minute to think over her words, so Toni acted with a kind of loving desperation and linked her arms about his bare neck.

'I love you so terribly, *señor*,' she whispered.

'Is that so?' He lay very still, but she could feel his heartbeats in accord with her own, beating through his skin until she felt that she breathed him, knew only him in all the city of Paris—all the world.

'Ah, Toni, Toni,' he groaned her name and suddenly he had her so close to him that only heaven could ever come between them. 'I want to take you as much as I want to keep you innocent and unhurt. You raise a storm in me, and if I unleashed it——'

'Oh, Luque, let it happen, darling, darling Luque! I shan't break like a toy—I'm a *woman*.'

'And I, Tonita, *adorada*, am a man.'

'I know you are.'

'Double your age, and experience.'

'So you keep telling me, *señor*.'

'But still controlled enough to end this before it begins.'

'You dare!'

'Toni, I begin to believe you're a young baggage.'

'Sister Imaculata certainly thought so. She tried to tame me with a scrubbing brush.'

'I shan't use anything that rough——' And with a laughing groan his mouth came down on her lips that were soft, curving, and sweet with giving.

'Toni, *querida*, be very sure.' He leaned on an elbow and looked down deeply into her eyes. 'I haven't been a good man, you know.'

'You'll improve, my darling Satan,' she smiled. 'It's being happy that makes people good, and I mean to make you the happiest man in the world.'

'Mmmm, I already begin to feel my wings spreading,' he murmured, wickedly, and once again their lips met with a joyous hunger.

Best Seller Romances

Romances you have loved

Mills & Boon Best Seller Romances are the love stories that have proved particularly popular with our readers. They really are "back by popular demand." These are the other titles to look out for this month.

FOLLOW A SHADOW
by Anne Hampson

All the bad blood of his wild Border forebears – the Evil Dewars, they had been called – flowed in the veins of Bren Dewar. He was hard, ruthless and overbearing – yet still timid Laura Vernon loved him. But even Laura was not prepared for the way Bren was planning to take over her life . . .

CUPBOARD LOVE
by Roberta Leigh

Miranda Jones was beautiful, witty and a professional cook. It was her cooking that led her to a meeting with wealthy young banker Blaize Jefferson. But cooking was not the way to his heart – for that was already given to someone else. But when that someone else came back into his life, Miranda was called on to help him – as cook and temporary fiancée. How Miranda wished the pretence could turn into reality!

THE WILDERNESS HUT
by Mary Wibberley

Eve Carrick was a rich girl who had only to lift her little finger to be waited on hand and foot. Garth Seton was the pilot she had hired to fly her about and generally make himself useful on a trip to Finland. But Garth Seton didn't jump to anyone's bidding . . .

Mills & Boon
the rose of romance

Best Seller Romances

Next month's best loved romances

Mills & Boon Best Seller Romances are the love stories that have proved particularly popular with our readers. These are the titles to look out for next month.

THE NIGHT OF THE COTILLION Janet Dailey
FORBIDDEN Anne Mather
THE SUN OF SUMMER Lilian Peake
THE LOVE THEME Margaret Way

Buy them from your usual paperback stockist, or write to: Mills & Boon Reader Service, P.O. Box 236, Thornton Rd, Croydon, Surrey CR9 3RU, England. Readers in South Africa-write to: Mills & Boon Reader Service of Southern Africa, Private Bag X3010, Randburg, 2125.

Mills & Boon
the rose of romance

Masquerade
Historical Romances

Intrigue
excitement
romance

THE CHIEFTAIN
by Caroline Martin

The young widow Isobel Carnegie is much sought after for he
beauty as well as her fortune. But when she is kidnapped by
the Highland Chieftain Hector MacLean, is he really only
interested in her money?

TO CATCH AN EARL
by Rosina Pyatt

The beautiful, and immensely wealthy, Miss Dominga
Romero-Browne is determined to marry the Earl of
Deversham. But the Earl's heart belongs to another, so how
can Dominga, once she is the Countess of Deversham, hope
to win more than a title?

Look out for these titles in your local paperback shop from
9th July 1982

Your chance to step into the past and re-live four love stories . . .

TAKE FOUR BOOKS FREE

An introduction to
The Masquerade Reader Service.

NO OBLIGATION.

HISTORICAL ROMANCES

To: The Masquerade Reader Service,
FREEPOST, PO Box 236, Croydon, Surrey CR9 9EL

Please send me *free and without obligation* the four latest Masquerade Historical
Romances and reserve a Reader Service subscription for me. If I decide to subscribe I
shall receive, following my free parcel of books, four new Historical Romances every
two months for £3.80 post and packing free. If I decide not to subscribe, I shall write to
you within 21 days, *but whatever I decide, the free books are mine to keep.* I understand that I
may cancel my subscription at any time, simply by writing to you. I am over 18 years
of age.

Please write in BLOCK CAPITALS

Name_____

Address_____

_____

_____ Post Code_____

Offer available in UK only. Overseas send for details.
SEND NO MONEY – TAKE NO RISKS. 7C2